**"I'm going to find out who did this,"
Harrison said. "I won't let anyone hurt
you, Honey."**

She started to say something but he stopped her.
"Shh." He pressed his finger to her lips to quiet her.
"I mean it. People in this town haven't been nice to
you and it's not right. I should have stood up for you
a long time ago, when we were kids."

A blush stained her face and she averted her eyes
as if bad memories had assaulted her.

"I'm sorry. I didn't mean to remind you of the past."

"I can't ever forget the past," Honey said. "Not until
we figure out if my father killed your sister."

Their gazes locked. Tension escalated. Emotions
and desires flamed between them.

She shivered and Harrison realized he'd wanted to
soothe and protect and touch her ever since he'd
seen her at the morgue.

No longer able to resist, he stroked her cheek with
the back of his thumb, then lowered his head and
kissed her.

# REDEMPTION AT HAWK'S LANDING

USA TODAY Bestselling Author

## RITA HERRON

To the fans of The Heroes of Horseshoe Creek series who asked for another family—meet the Hawks!

Recycling programs for this product may not exist in your area.

ISBN-13: 978-0-373-75716-9

Redemption at Hawk's Landing

Copyright © 2017 by Rita B. Herron

**Printed in U.S.A.**

*USA TODAY* bestselling author **Rita Herron** wrote her first book when she was twelve but didn't think real people grew up to be writers. Now she writes so she doesn't have to get a real job. A former kindergarten teacher and workshop leader, she traded storytelling to kids for writing romance, and now she writes romantic comedies and romantic suspense. Rita lives in Georgia with her family. She loves to hear from readers, so please visit her website, ritaherron.com.

## Books by Rita Herron

### Harlequin Intrigue

#### Badge of Justice

*Redemption at Hawk's Landing*

#### The Heroes of Horseshoe Creek

*Lock, Stock and McCullen*
*McCullen's Secret Son*
*Roping Ray McCullen*
*Warrior Son*
*The Missing McCullen*
*The Last McCullen*

#### Bucking Bronc Lodge

*Certified Cowboy*
*Cowboy in the Extreme*
*Cowboy to the Max*
*Cowboy Cop*
*Native Cowboy*
*Ultimate Cowboy*

*Cold Case at Camden Crossing*
*Cold Case at Carlton's Canyon*
*Cold Case at Cobra Creek*
*Cold Case in Cherokee Crossing*

Visit the Author Profile page at Harlequin.com for more titles.

# CAST OF CHARACTERS

*Sheriff Harrison Hawk*—Guilt ridden over his sister's disappearance eighteen years ago, Harrison must investigate the murder of the man he suspected is responsible. But can he protect his heart when old wounds and desires draw him to Granger's beautiful daughter, Honey?

*Honey Granger*—Tainted by the suspicions about her father, Honey wants the truth. But finding it means teaming up with Harrison Hawk, the man she had a crush on as a teen—the man whose mother hates her.

*Chrissy Hawk*—Her disappearance tore the Hawk family apart. What happened to her?

*Special Agent Lucas Hawk*—He blames himself for his sister's disappearance because he stood by while one of his friends bullied her.

*Dexter Hawk*—He fought with Chrissy the night she disappeared and told her to get lost—and then she did...

*Brayden Hawk*—He believes it's his fault his sister was lost because he convinced Chrissy to sneak out with him the night she went missing.

*Ava Hawk*—Chrissy's mother suspected Waylon Granger of abducting and killing her precious daughter. But she has her own secrets...

*Reverend Langley*—Does the local preacher know more than he's saying about Chrissy's disappearance?

*Geoffrey Williams*—Did this respected town council member do something to Chrissy eighteen years ago?

*Elden Lynch*—Is he as harmless as he seems?

*Mrs. Lynch*—She will do anything to protect her son, who has a mental disability, and keep him away from Honey Granger.

# Chapter One

The dead man lay sprawled on the mountain ridge at Dead Man's Bluff, his eyes blank, his arm twisted at an odd angle.

He'd probably broken it in the fall. Blood matted his graying hair from where he'd hit the rock as he'd gone over the edge of the ridge.

Sheriff Harrison Hawk cursed. Dammit, he'd recognized him immediately.

Waylon Granger.

The man his mother blamed for his sister's disappearance eighteen years ago. They'd never been able to prove he was at fault, though.

And now he was dead; they might never know the truth.

Curiosity over what had happened nagged at Harrison. Granger was a known drunk, and a mean one. Even his daughter, Honey, had left home after high school graduation to escape the bastard.

What was Granger doing here at Dead Man's Bluff?

This was the teenage hangout—just as years ago he and his friends had been drawn to the swimming hole and dark mines with the mysterious ghost stories that surrounded them, the local high schoolers still frequented it.

The two thirteen-year-old boys who'd called in

the body sat hunched by Granger's rusty pickup, their young faces etched in horror.

The scent of death hit Harrison, the summer heat accentuating it.

Memories of the night his little sister, Chrissy, had gone missing bombarded him. The years since hadn't dulled the pain or trauma. It felt as if it had happened yesterday.

He was seventeen at the time and supposed to babysit his siblings that night while his parents attended a party. Instead, he'd sneaked out to meet his buddies at this very place.

He inhaled sharply. He'd thought Lucas, fifteen, would watch their thirteen-year-old brother, Dexter, eleven-year-old Brayden and their ten-year-old sister, Chrissy. But Lucas had a friend visiting and hadn't noticed when Chrissy and his youngest brother, Brayden, sneaked out. Dexter claimed he and Chrissy had argued because he was playing video games and she kept interrupting. Brayden and Chrissy rode their bikes to the bluff to see what Harrison was up to.

While they were exploring, Brayden tripped and sprained his ankle. Chrissy went to get help. Brayden thought she'd run to Honey Granger's, but Honey denied seeing her that night.

The sheriff organized a search party, and they'd searched the mines and town and dragged the swimming hole. But they hadn't found her.

Someone claimed they'd seen Granger's truck

drive by, casting suspicion on him. Granger denied picking Chrissy up or having any contact with her.

Desperate for a big-sister role model, Chrissy had taken a shine to Granger's daughter, Honey. But Harrison's mother didn't like Honey and had forbidden her from hanging out with the teenager.

Honey's father didn't allow Honey friends or visitors, so Harrison's mother suggested that the man had caught Chrissy on their property, lost his temper and done something to her.

The boys' voices sounded from Granger's truck and dragged Harrison back to reality. The taller one stood and walked toward him, his eyes wide with fear. "C-can we go home now, Sheriff?"

Harrison felt for the boy. He and his friend were only kids and had no business being out here by themselves. The mines and bluff were dangerous.

Hopefully they'd learned their lesson.

Unfortunately neither had seen anyone else at the bluff. They'd been horsing around, throwing rocks off the ridge when they noticed the vultures, then spotted Granger's body on the ledge below.

"Yeah, but be careful. If you think of anything else you saw, call me."

The boy nodded, then jogged over to his bicycle. His friend joined him, then the two of them began pedaling as fast as they could to get away. Tonight they'd probably be glad to go home to their parents.

A siren wailed in the distance, indicating the rescue team and crime team were approaching. Once they recovered Granger's body, they'd transport it to the morgue for an autopsy.

Although most likely Granger had been drunk and had simply slipped and fallen, Harrison had a job to do. Whether or not he liked the man didn't matter.

He had to verify that his death was accidental.

His stomach knotted. He also had to call Honey and deliver the news that her father was gone. It was one conversation he dreaded.

HONEY GRANGER WIPED perspiration from her forehead, the Austin summer heat stifling as she studied her latest project—a brick ranch built in 1960 that she was renovating.

The scent of dust and old weathered wood blended with the hint of new pine she'd bought to replace the rotting boards on the kitchen floor.

Adrenaline pumped through her. Taking dilapidated, run-down houses that had been left for dead and refurbishing them was challenging but stimulating. She loved transforming the ruins into something beautiful, and had built a successful business out of it.

She'd been trying to do the same for herself for years—take the battered girl who'd run from Tumbleweed, Texas, and make her into something to be proud of. Sometimes she thought she'd succeeded.

Other times she felt like the tainted teenager with the thrift store clothes and shady family, who'd run away when the gossip and rumors became too crushing.

Her contractor and business partner, Jared North, strode toward her, swinging his sledgehammer.

Today was his favorite part—demo day.

He tilted his hard hat. "You want that wall between the kitchen and living room knocked out?"

Honey nodded. "Everyone wants open concept these days, to be able to see their friends and family while they cook and entertain."

"Got it," Jared said. "It's load bearing, though, so we'll have to install a support beam."

"It'll be worth it." Honey stepped back, mentally picturing the reconfigured design of the kitchen. "With the wall gone, we can install upper and lower cabinets, and build a large center island, maybe from reclaimed wood, for more prep space and storage beneath." She walked over and examined the fireplace. "Remove the Sheetrock. My guess is there's shiplap below it. Exposing it will add character to the space."

"Yes, ma'am."

Honey laughed at his mock salute. The planning and design stage, she was in charge. But when it came to the actual construction details and labor, Jared took command and she saluted him.

"How about the bathrooms?" Jared asked.

"We're gutting them." The outdated tiles and flooring had to go. She just hoped they didn't find water damage or mold.

Her phone buzzed at her hip, and she checked the number. The area code wasn't Austin's, but it seemed familiar. It took her a moment to realize the location.

Tumbleweed.

Nerves fluttered in her belly. The sheriff's office.

Fear and anger resurfaced quickly. Good grief, she'd recognize that number anywhere. What had her father done now? He'd been arrested for public drunkenness, disorderly conduct and driving under the influence when she lived at home. And she'd had to bail him out.

But she'd cut off contact when she'd left town and told Sheriff Dunar not to bother calling her when he locked her father up again.

The phone buzzed again. Jared frowned. "Aren't you going to answer that?"

Honey shook her head. She didn't give a damn if her father was in trouble. He had shamed her enough in high school. She'd moved away years ago to escape the stigma.

She refused to let him taint her newfound life here in Austin.

The phone settled, and she and Jared walked through the rest of the house. She pointed out her plans—a new window here, French doors off the living room to open up to the patio they were re-surfacing, removal of all the popcorn ceiling, bathroom remodel.

Her phone buzzed again just as they finished. The same number.

Damn.

"What's wrong, Honey?" Jared asked.

She bit the inside of her cheek. "Nothing." She snatched up the phone. "I guess I'd better take this." She'd tell Sheriff Dunar to lose her number and never bother her again.

Her lungs tightened as she hurried outside to the backyard for air. Just the thought of her father made her feel dirty.

Ready to get the call over with, she pressed Connect. "Hello."

A heartbeat of silence passed. "Is this Honey Granger?"

Honey heaved a breath. It didn't sound like Sheriff Dunar. "Yes, who is this?"

"Harrison Hawk… I'm sheriff now."

Honey swallowed hard. Harrison Hawk was sheriff of Tumbleweed?

Good God. She'd had such a crush on him when she was younger. But then his little sister went missing, and her hellish life became a real nightmare when her father became a suspect.

"Harrison?" Honey rubbed her damp forehead, wiping at the perspiration. "How did you get my number? Why—"

"Just listen, Honey. It's important."

She leaned her back against a sawtooth tree and

waited, but her gaze homed in on the sagging porch and rotting awning of her renovation project.

"I have bad news," he said in a gruff voice. "It's about your father."

Was there any other kind of news where he was concerned? "What has he done now?"

Another tense moment passed, then Harrison cleared his throat. "I'm sorry, Honey. I hate to have to tell you this, but he's dead."

Honey's legs buckled, and she felt herself sliding to the ground just like the rotting exterior of her latest project.

SEVERAL TENSE SECONDS passed as Harrison gave Honey time to absorb the news.

A rescue team and the medical examiner sped up the winding road to the clearing at the top of the hill and screeched to a halt.

"Honey, are you still there?"

The rescue team climbed from their vehicle, followed by the ME. Harrison waved them over to the ridge and pointed out the body.

"Honey?"

"I'm here," she said in a strained voice.

"I'm sorry," he said again. "I just thought you'd want to know." Or maybe not. She hadn't returned to Tumbleweed in years. He didn't know if she'd spoken to her father recently or if they'd communicated at all since she'd left.

"How? His drinking?"

"I can't say for sure until the autopsy."

Another strained silence. She was obviously in shock.

"I'll transport the body to the morgue," he said, hating to sound callous but he didn't know what else to say. Better to just stick to business. "I didn't know if you wanted to come back and make arrangements—"

A heavy sigh. "I'll let you know when I get there."

"All right." He watched as the rescue team anchored a harness so they could climb down and bring up the body. "If there's anything I can do, just let me know."

Honey murmured, "Okay." A second later the phone went silent, leaving him wondering if she'd been alone or with someone. He should have asked before he dropped the bomb.

But he and Honey hadn't exactly been friends when she lived in Tumbleweed. Worse, his sister's disappearance had cast a dark cloud over both their families.

The rescue workers' voices jerked him from his thoughts, a reminder he needed to focus on the job. He strode to the edge of the bluff and looked down.

One of the workers was kneeling by Granger's body.

Harrison used his camera phone to take pictures before the men moved it. The ME stepped up beside him.

"What happened?" Dr. Weinberger asked.

Harrison shrugged. "Don't know. Looks like he fell. A couple of kids called it in. I took their statements and let them go home. They were pretty shaken."

The ME glanced around the area. "They see anyone else up here?"

Harrison shook his head. "No. They were throwing rocks off the ridge when they saw vultures circling over Granger's body. See that blood on the back of his head?"

Harrison nodded. Granger lay facedown, arms at odd angles. "Looks like he broke his arms trying to brace his fall."

"Yes, it does," the ME said. "He fell face forward. So how did he get the gash on the back of his head?"

The air around Harrison stirred, bringing the scent of impending rain and the whisper of the ghosts the locals gossiped about. Some said it was the miners screaming when the mine had collapsed on top of them.

Others justified the eerie whistle of the wind as just that—the wind rolling off the mountain ridge.

The ME's words echoed in Harrison's ears. Granger fell face forward. The back of his head was one bloody mess.

His gaze met the doctor's as he realized the implication. "Damn. He didn't just fall, did he? He was murdered."

# Chapter Two

Honey ignored the grief stabbing at her the rest of the day as she finalized plans for the house renovation. She left the project in her partner's hands, trusting him with implementing her design, then drove back to the small Craftsman-style bungalow she'd bought two years ago.

This was home sweet home. Her happy place.

Here she was safe from her past. From the rumors and gossip and the nastiness that had been her life.

She had no idea how long she'd be in Tumbleweed. Only as long as it took to address her father's will and handle his burial. She definitely would not give him a memorial service.

It wasn't like anyone would attend if she did.

Her father hadn't been a popular man in Tumbleweed when she lived there. She couldn't imagine he'd made friends since.

She took a deep breath as she entered her home, savoring the cozy interior she'd personally designed to her taste. She liked the farmhouse, shabby-chic look, but avoided anything reminiscent of her childhood home.

Memories bombarded her—sleeping in a room with no heat, with raggedy quilts piled so thickly on her that she couldn't turn over. The furnace in the den barely kept that room warm. The summers were hot and stale, the rooms reeking of smoke, rotting wood and booze.

She blinked back tears, walked to her bedroom and dragged out a suitcase. The earthy tones mingled with slate blue in the room to soothe her nerves after a long day.

But as she gathered jeans, shirts, boots and a couple of skirts, the memory of the wind jarring the windowpanes in her father's house taunted her as if she was standing in that old house.

She would be soon.

Scrubbing her hand over her eyes to blot out the tears and wipe her emotions away, she braced herself. She wouldn't let that place or her father's death get to her.

Not ever again.

In her mind, he'd died a long time ago. This visit was just a formality, then she could erase him, Tumbleweed and its residents from her life forever.

ANXIETY KNOTTED HARRISON's shoulders as he parked at the morgue the next morning. Honey Granger was meeting him here.

He hadn't slept the night before for stewing over the fact that she was coming back to town. He didn't exactly know why that thought unnerved him, but it did.

His first instinct had been to call his family together and relay the news about Granger's death, but he'd kept the information between the ME, his deputy, Mitchell Bronson, and himself.

Telling his mother and brothers would dredge up all the pain again.

He also wanted to verify the cause of death. Everyone in town knew that his mother hated Granger, which would no doubt lay suspicion on her. Truthfully on his entire family.

He wasn't ready to deal with that suspicion or to throw his mother and siblings into the line of fire.

Sweat beaded on his forehead as he climbed from his SUV onto the hot asphalt and walked toward the hospital. The morgue and ME's office were located in the basement. Already the noonday sun was beating down full force and the temperature was climbing.

His phone buzzed. Dr. Weinberger. He punched Connect. "Sheriff Hawk."

"Harrison, Honey Granger is here."

"I'll be there in a couple of minutes. I just parked." He ended the call and took a deep breath as he entered the hospital. The image of Honey Granger at sixteen with her golden-blond hair, big brown eyes and long legs made his gut tighten.

As a teenager she'd been pretty but homely, with her ragged secondhand clothes. The popular girls had been mean to her, and the boys had joked about getting into her pants. Two football players had made a bet to see who could screw her first.

A foul taste settled in Harrison's mouth. She had definitely gotten a bad rap.

Oddly his little sister was the one who'd stood up for Honey instead of him. He wasn't proud of that.

Chrissy had liked Honey's flashy clothes, jewelry and makeup.

But their mother had forbidden her from hanging out with the girl, saying Honey was too old to be friends with Chrissy and that Honey looked like a tramp.

When Honey left town abruptly after high school, rumors surfaced that she'd gotten pregnant and had gone away to have the baby.

He'd hoped that wasn't true, that she'd found a better life.

The air-conditioning hit him as he entered the hospital, stark against the blazing summer heat. He strode to the elevator and rode down to the basement, the scent of cleaner and antiseptic was strong as he walked down the hall to the ME's office.

The receptionist waved him in. When he'd phoned Honey, she'd obviously been shocked at the news of her father's death and hadn't said much.

He had no idea what to expect today. Granger was her father and the only family she had left. He was surprised she hadn't asked for more details, but everyone reacted differently to bad news. She probably would be asking now.

And he needed to find out the answers.

He knocked then eased open the door to Weinberger's office. Dr. Weinberger stood and nodded in greeting, then Harrison's gaze fell on Honey.

The teenager with the too-flashy clothes had disappeared.

This woman wore jeans with a silky-looking deep blue top and strappy heels that made her legs look endlessly long. Her hair was just as blond and golden looking, her big brown eyes smoldering hot, sensual, like liquid pools a man could drown in.

His gut clenched. Dammit she was…beautiful. In a wholesome, almost-innocent way.

"Honey?" He offered his hand.

Her hand trembled as she placed her slender palm in his. Heat rippled through him at her touch.

A wary look flashed in her eyes, and she rubbed her palm on her jeans as if she'd felt it, too. Then her soft lips pressed into a thin line, and a frown darkened her face.

"We were waiting on you," Dr. Weinberger said. "I explained to Honey that she doesn't need to make an ID, that we recognized her father, and DNA confirms it's Waylon. But if she wants to see him, that's fine, too."

Harrison arched a brow, waiting on Honey's response. He needed time to get his reaction to her under control.

Their past was way too complicated for him to be attracted to her now.

HONEY QUICKLY AVERTED her gaze from Harrison.

Good heavens. She'd thought he was cute when he was seventeen, but he was so handsome now he could bring a woman to her knees.

He'd morphed into a mountain of a man with big, broad shoulders, a muscular body, the deepest amber eyes she'd ever seen and an all-gruff, masculine exterior. His tanned skin and dark hair accentuated his high cheekbones, square jaw and the cleft in his chin.

He had dimples, too, when he smiled, although that smile had disappeared after his sister went missing. It was still gone.

In fact, his frown suggested he found her lacking.

His mother's hateful words had been imprinted in her brain forever. "You're trash, Honey Granger. You're not welcome at Hawk's Landing. My daughter is *not* going to associate with the likes of you."

"Have you decided on arrangements?" Harrison asked, jarring her from the painful memories.

Honey shrugged. "According to Daddy's lawyer, Truitt Bennings, my father wanted to be cremated." She was surprised that her father had a will, but grateful he did. He'd left the house to her. Owning it outright would make it easier to sell.

She didn't intend to stay in this town any longer than necessary.

"I can call the crematory for you if you want," Dr. Weinberger offered.

"Thank you," Honey said. "I'd appreciate that."

Dr. Weinberger gave her a sympathetic smile. "Do you want to see him now?"

Did she? No. When she'd left town, she'd sworn never to see or speak to him again.

But some inner voice beckoned her to at least say goodbye. After all, he was her father. And he hadn't deserted her as her mother had, although some could argue that drinking himself into a stupor was his way of abandoning her and reality.

She stood, lifting her chin and putting on a brave face. "Yes. Let's get it over with."

Harrison and the doctor exchanged an odd look, but neither commented. She almost asked what was going on, but decided they'd probably discussed her before she'd arrived. Gossip in small towns was hard to overcome. For all she knew, everyone in Tumbleweed knew of her arrival.

She lifted her chin. Dammit, she didn't care what the people here thought of her anymore. She'd made herself a new life, and she was proud of who she'd become.

Still, their quiet looks made her uneasy and reminded her of the reason she hated Tumbleweed.

Dr. Weinberger led her from the office through a set of double doors past a room labeled Autopsy, then into a smaller space. She took a deep breath to brace herself, then followed him over to a steel gurney. The room was so cold that she shivered.

Her father lay beneath the draped cloth.

The ME stepped to the opposite side of the table. "Are you ready, Ms. Granger?"

She nodded.

He pulled the cloth away from her father's face, but she didn't react. It was as if she was looking at a stranger, someone she'd met years ago, someone who hadn't meant anything to her. Age had turned his hair gray, carved deep lines in his craggy face, and he'd lost weight. The yellowish-gray pallor of his skin coupled with the bruises on his face looked stark beneath the harsh lighting.

"What happened?" she asked. She'd assumed it was the liquor, but his face looked like he'd been in a bar fight.

The doctor shifted. Beside her, Harrison's breath puffed into the air. "I found him at Dead Man's Bluff."

Honey looked at him for confirmation. "Why was he there?"

"I don't know," Harrison said.

"How did he die?" Honey asked.

"Cause of death was head trauma," Dr. Weinberger said.

"So he was drunk and fell?" Honey said, disgusted.

A tense second passed. Harrison cleared his throat. "He didn't simply fall, Honey. It looks like he was struck by a rock then pushed over the edge."

Shock bolted through Honey. "You mean someone murdered him?"

"I'm sorry," Harrison said. "But yes, it looks that way."

Now she understood the odd looks between the men.

Her mind began to race. Her father hadn't had any friends in town. A lot of people didn't like him, but no one hated him enough to kill him.

Except...

Her gaze met Harrison's. Except for his family.

HARRISON SAW THE wheels in Honey's mind turning. She was jumping to the same conclusion that everyone else would—that one of his family members might be responsible.

"Do you know who pushed him?" she asked, tactfully avoiding an accusation.

He didn't have the answer to that question.

"Not yet."

He would find the truth, though. That was his damn job.

"Would you like a few minutes alone?" Dr. Weinberger asked.

Another tense heartbeat passed. Honey twisted her hands together, looking fragile for a moment, then she gave a slight nod.

"Let us know if you need anything," the ME said.

For some reason, Harrison was reluctant to leave her alone. She'd grown up in a house filled with turmoil. Had suffered at the hands of her mother and father. Had left nearly two decades ago.

And now she'd traveled back here alone to say goodbye to the man who'd failed her.

Compassion for her made him reach out and squeeze her arm. "Are you okay?"

A sad smile curved her mouth. "Of course. I'll just be a minute."

Harrison nodded, then followed the medical examiner into the hallway. Worried about her, he turned and watched her through the window in the door, unable to leave.

"She seems to be handling it okay," Dr. Weinberger said in a low voice.

Either that or she was good at acting. He had a feeling Honey Granger had done a lot of that over the years—pretending the rumors and gossip hadn't hurt her. But deep-seated pain colored her eyes.

He had the sudden need to make things right for her. To strip her of the anguish she was suffering.

But he didn't have a clue as to how to do that.

Besides, she would probably leave town as soon as she handled the details surrounding her father's death, the cremation and possibly the sale of his house. Unless she decided to move back and live in it.

A sardonic chuckle rumbled in his throat. He didn't see that happening. Ever.

"Did you find any forensics?" Harrison asked.

Weinberger crossed his arms. "Slivers of rock and dirt were embedded in the back of Granger's head where he was struck. My guess is that he was hit with a rock from the bluff."

Harrison shifted. "That would imply the murder wasn't premeditated, that something happened on that ledge that triggered the other party to attack."

He'd have to go back to the bluff, look for that rock, see if there were fingerprints on it.

"Anything else?" Harrison asked.

"Dirt under his fingernails and a short brown hair."

Harrison gave a nod. "Send it to the lab. That hair may belong to our killer."

# Chapter Three

Her father had been murdered.

That fact echoed in Honey's head as if someone was pounding the words inside her skull.

Who had killed her father? And why?

Emotions welled in her chest as she studied his cold body. Eighteen years had aged him, but the alcohol had intensified the process, adding another ten years. The bruises and contusions on his face looked stark beneath the lights. His skin was a sallow yellow, lips a bluish purple, eyes closed as if… as if he was at peace.

Maybe he finally was. She'd never understood the reason he drank so heavily, why his moods changed erratically, and she'd blamed herself. He missed her mother… He hadn't wanted a child… He didn't know how to raise a daughter, especially alone… She'd been a bad kid.

On a more rational level, as an adult, she realized he'd battled inner demons that she knew nothing about; that alcoholism was a disease. But his behavior and his rejection had hurt.

Tears pricked at her eyes, and she ached with a sudden longing to go back in time. To a time when she was little, and he'd carried her fishing at the pond. He'd surprised her that day by packing a picnic and taking her on a canoe ride. For a couple of hours she'd felt like she had a real family. He'd taught her how to cast a fishing rod and laughed when she'd been squeamish over baiting her own hook with worms.

Yet that precious memory had been ruined when he'd pulled out a bottle of whiskey, consumed most of it and passed out in the sun. She'd fished alone and played at the edge of the water and pretended everything was okay. She'd gotten good at pretending.

But then night set in and the wilderness had seemed vast and lonely and…creepy. She'd been terrified as darkness encroached and the howl of coyotes had echoed around her. She'd shaken him to wake him up so they could go home, but he'd been belligerent, cursed her then backhanded her for crying.

He'd also been so inebriated that he'd woven all over the road and nearly crashed into another car head-on. He'd blamed that on her, as well.

She shivered. When they'd finally made it home, she ran into her bedroom, locked the door and hid there all night and half of the next day, too afraid to come out and face his wrath.

Honey straightened, banishing the memory to the attic of her mind with the other troubling ones that she'd packed away. No use dwelling on them. You had to play with the cards you'd been dealt.

She'd accepted her father for what he was long ago, but a sliver of hope had remained that one day he might change and she'd have the loving, caring father she'd always wanted.

Now any chance of that was lost forever.

Resigned and swallowing back tears, she placed her hand against his cheek. His skin felt leathery, rough, cold in death. She had an insane urge to kiss his cheek, but refrained.

Instead she whispered, "Goodbye, Daddy," and left the room, shutting out this image and the pain as the door closed behind her.

HARRISON CONTEMPLATED HIS conversation with the ME. If they identified Granger's killer, he could solve this case quickly. Then Honey could leave and take her tempting, pretty little butt with her.

Harrison phoned the crime scene investigator and spoke with the lead CSI, Roger Watkins. "Did you find any forensics at the bluff where Waylon Granger's body was discovered?"

"Nothing on the ledge. No definitive footprints, either. We did collect a button. Looks like it came from a flannel shirt. Not Granger's and no print on it."

"Hell, it could have been there no telling how long."

But he had to revisit the crime scene. If Granger had been hit by a rock, the perp could have tossed it far enough away so CSI hadn't found it. That rock could be key evidence.

The door opened and Honey appeared. Harrison's gut tightened at the strain on her face.

"I should be finished with the autopsy by tomorrow, then I'll contact the crematorium," Dr. Weinberger said.

"Thanks." Honey folded her arms around her waist. "I'll be at my father's house for a couple of days. I'm going to see what needs to be done to get it on the market." She lifted her gaze to Harrison, a world of old hurts flashing in her big eyes, then directed her comment to the ME. "Harrison—the sheriff—has my number if you need me."

Dr. Weinberger gave a quick nod. "Yes, ma'am."

"I'll walk you out, Honey," Harrison said as she started toward the door.

She stiffened as he fell into step beside her, and they walked down the hall and rode the elevator in silence. Even though the heat was stifling, Harrison welcomed the fresh air as they stepped outside. Honey's shoulders relaxed, too.

He followed her to a white minivan emblazoned with a graphic of a house and a company name, Honey's Home Makeovers.

"You own your own business?" Harrison asked.

The anger on Honey's face dissipated slightly and a small smile titled her lips. "Yes. Don't sound so surprised."

Her defensive tone made him feel like a heel. "I didn't mean it like that." He shifted on the balls of his feet, hoping she'd elaborate but she didn't.

The familiar wary expression returned. "You said my father was pushed over that ledge. Do you have any idea who did it?"

Her gaze met his, the past once again creating an impenetrable barrier between them.

"I'm investigating." He jammed his hands in his pockets.

She studied him for a moment, her lips pressed into a thin line. He wanted to see that smile again, and found himself wondering if she had someone special in her life, someone she graced with that smile all the time.

If she did, the guy was a lucky man.

She hit the key fob to unlock her van, and he closed his fingers around the handle to open the door. His arm brushed hers, and she startled, then stepped away from him as if he'd burned her.

"Sorry," he murmured.

She shrugged as if she realized she'd overreacted. Then she slid into the driver's seat.

He caught the door with his hand before she could close it. "Did you and your father stay in touch?"

She heaved a breath, filled with wary resignation, then shook her head. "No, I haven't spoken to him in years. Why? You don't think I had something to do with his death?"

He should consider that theory, but no, it hadn't occurred to him. "No," he said honestly.

"Good," she said sharply. "Because I have a life in Austin, Harrison. I have my own business and love what I do. When I left here, I left everything behind. That included my father." She clenched the steering wheel with a white-knuckle grip. "No matter how much I despised him, there's no way I would have jeopardized my career to get back at him, especially now." A sad expression washed over her face. "He wasn't worth it."

She started the engine, pressed the gas and sped from the parking lot.

Harrison stood for a moment, absorbing her statement. Sad that she didn't feel more grief toward the old man. But then again, Granger didn't deserve it.

He glanced toward the mountain. Remembering that the murder weapon was most likely a rock, he walked to his SUV, climbed in and drove to Dead Man's Bluff. He parked, then scanned the area, tormented by the memory of that fateful night Chrissy went missing. The fact that her body hadn't been found should have given him hope that she was alive, but…he knew the odds.

Was her disappearance somehow tied to Waylon Granger's murder? He didn't see how it could be.

But he had to know.

He pulled on latex gloves and climbed from his SUV. The sun beat down on him as he combed the parking area and weeds beside it. He searched the overgrown bushes flanking the old mine, and the weeds jutting up by the swimming hole.

Nothing.

Of course the killer could have tossed the rock

into the swimming hole and it could be under water. The wind whistled from the cave, that ghostly sound that stirred the rumors surrounding the place, and he retrieved his flashlight from the truck.

Determined to explore all possible avenues before diving into the swimming hole, he crept inside the entrance to the mine. It was dark as hell inside, cold, and smelled of wet moss, dirt and decay. The scent of urine was almost overpowering, suggesting that curiosity seekers not only ventured inside but used it as a bathroom, too.

Ignoring the stench, he raked the flashlight along the wall and searched the floor. The opening was clear. Cigarette butts, beer bottles and evidence of discarded drug paraphernalia.

He picked up a stick and raked away some of the trash then made his way to the corner where he found an old sleeping bag, two empty tin cans that had held beans and a metal coffee mug. Had someone been living inside?

He shone the light along the wall and spotted a small cluster of rocks in a circular pattern. Burned sticks lay in a pile of ashes in the middle.

His light illuminated the corner of the pile, and he noticed a rock shoved into the debris. He stooped down and raked away the ashes with a stick.

It definitely was a rock, a sharp, jagged one. He peered closer. Something red stained the side of the stone.

He pulled the rock from the pile and examined

it. It was almost as large as his hand and could have been used as a weapon.

He sniffed the red substance. It was sticky and held a metallic odor—definitely blood.

~~Granger's?~~ He'd have it tested.

Pulse jumping, he carried it from the cave, ~~bagged~~ it and stowed it in his truck. If there were prints on it, he might be able to nail the killer.

His gut tightened with dread.

He hadn't yet told his family about Granger's death. It was time he did.

He glanced at the rock on the seat of his truck with trepidation. He just hoped he didn't find one of their prints on that rock.

HONEY PASSED THE sheriff's office as she drove through Tumbleweed. She couldn't believe Harrison Hawk was sheriff. She'd expected him to leave this small town for something bigger and better. Harrison was smart, had been popular, had girls swooning over him.

His bad-boy sexy, flirty ways had been appealing. But after his sister disappeared, he'd become angry, moody and sullen.

His close-knit family had fallen apart.

Several mothers and their children played in the park at the edge of town where they'd added splash pads for the kids to cool off in the summer heat. Her heart squeezed as a little girl in pigtails with pink ribbons flying in the wind ran toward her mother and threw her arms around her.

Ribbons… Chrissy had loved ribbons in her hair and had collected a box of assorted colors.

Honey turned down the side street that led to Lower Tumbleweed, the street where her father lived. Technically the area was named Lower Tumbleweed because it sat in the lower valley. Although the name held another connotation, implying the families who lived there were lower-class. The families on the street were poor—the children received free lunches and free dental care, and they lived off food stamps.

Taunts from other kids about Lower Tumbleweed echoed in her head.

God, how she'd hated the cruel comments. Had hated that the kids at school knew so much about her. Worse, that the gossip about her mother being a tramp and her father a drunk were true.

At least her best friend at the time, Cora Zimmerman, had a mother who worked hard for a living. Not that Cora hadn't gotten teased, too, but at least her mother's job at the hair salon had been reputable.

She hadn't thought about Cora in a long time and wondered where she was now.

The street sign for her father's road had been run over and lay on the ground. Tire tracks marred the faded green metal. She knew the turn, though, and made it, her throat filling with disgust when she spotted the dilapidated, run-down houses and yards.

The houses had been small and worn eighteen years ago. Weather and lack of care had sent them downhill. Porches were sagging, boards rotting, paint peeling off, concrete driveways cracking, shutters dangling askew.

Weeds and dead bushes choked the yards, and debris from a recent storm littered what had once been grass. Most of the houses were vacant now, and a couple were boarded up as if they'd been condemned.

Her father's sat like an eyesore at the end of the street. The once-white wood had yellowed, and her father had substituted a lone brick to replace the broken steps to the porch. She sighed as she parked, and ran a hand through her hair.

She bought houses like this and completely renovated them, turning them into showcases. For a brief second an image of gorgeous little bungalows filled her vision. She could make this neighborhood into something to be proud of.

But every house needed to be gutted.

Sweat beaded on her neck as she climbed from the van.

No. She would not think about renovating the neighborhood. She didn't intend to stay here a minute longer than necessary. And she sure as hell didn't care if someone bulldozed every house on the street.

Tomorrow she'd talk to the local real estate agent and see if any investors were interested in the properties.

But tonight she had to stay here.

The thought sent dread through her. How was she going to sleep in this nasty place? It had been bad enough as a child before she'd known better.

She should have booked a room at the local inn, but she hadn't wanted to announce her arrival or come face-to-face with anyone else from her past.

Squaring her shoulders, she decided to check out the inside first. If it was unlivable, she'd try the inn.

Weeds clawed at her legs as she walked up to the porch. She climbed the makeshift brick step, then dodged holes in the floor as she crossed to the door. She jiggled it and it opened easily, then she stepped inside.

Nausea flooded her as her childhood rushed back. Images of her parents fighting hit her, along with the strong odor of cigarettes and booze.

It was a gut job. The threadbare sofa and chair her father had had when she lived here was falling apart. Cigarette ashes and empty liquor bottles testified to the fact that he hadn't changed his ways.

The kitchen was outdated, the cabinets sad looking, the Formica kitchen table and counters greasy and splattered with food stains.

Anger at her father for letting the place reach

such disrepair railed inside her. She'd seen worse on jobs, but this had once been her home, albeit a dysfunctional one, but at least it hadn't been filthy. Because she had cleaned it.

She passed the kitchen, then stopped in the hallway in front of her father's bedroom. The faded chenille spread remained, stained and dotted with cigarette burns. The metal bed was rusty, the curtains dingy, her father's work boots and clothes piled on a chair in the corner.

She forced herself to go into her old room. He hadn't changed the pink-and-white-gingham bedspread or curtains. Her teddy bear and dolls still sat on the shelf on the wall. She spotted the jewelry box she'd gotten for Christmas the year before her mother left, picked it up and sank onto the bed.

The springs creaked beneath her weight. Her mother had loved costume jewelry and had given Honey some of her pieces when she'd grown tired of them. Honey had called them her treasures and had played dress up in them, pretending to be glamorous.

A bitter chuckle rumbled from her chest.

She'd never been glamorous. Instead her attempts at dressing up her homely clothes as a teenager had only made her look cheap. No wonder Harrison's mother hadn't wanted Chrissy around her.

Unable to resist, she opened the jewelry box to see what was left of the costume jewelry.

Instead her heart leaped.

On top of the pop beads and clunky gold-and-rhinestone pieces lay a yellow ribbon.

Nausea churned in her stomach.

Chrissy had been wearing yellow ribbons the night she'd disappeared.

# Chapter Four

Honey draped the shiny bright yellow satin across her hand. An image of Chrissy's pigtails, tied with yellow ribbons, flashed behind her eyes.

Little Chrissy singing, "You are my sunshine, my only sunshine," as she skipped across the yard.

One day it would be yellow ribbons, the next day purple or red or blue.

Sometimes she wore ribbons of different colors and called them her rainbow hair.

She had been such a happy kid, all smiles and singing and curiosity. She had sneaked over to Honey's one day and asked Honey to show her how to wear makeup. Honey had thought it was sweet. Since the little girl only had brothers, she'd figured Chrissy needed a female in her life to teach her girl things.

In spite of Chrissy's pleas for layers of blush, eye shadow and lipstick, Honey had brushed her cheeks with a light powder, applied a pale pink gloss on her lips, then a very faint dusting of sparkly white eye shadow. Chrissy had thought she was beautiful.

But Chrissy's mother had stormed over to Honey's that night and ordered her to stay away from Chrissy. Mrs. Hawk finished by saying she didn't intend to allow Honey to make Chrissy look like a tramp.

Tears blurred Honey's eyes. She'd realized then that the gossip about her mother and father extended to her, and that she would never fit into the same social circle as people like Harrison Hawk and his family.

She'd also made up her mind to leave town as soon as she was old enough to get a job.

And she had.

She blinked to clear her vision and the memory. The yellow ribbon mocked her with questions, though.

How had it gotten in Honey's jewelry box?

If Chrissy was wearing this ribbon the night she disappeared, that meant whoever had killed her must have taken it. Which made it even more curious as to how it had gotten in her own jewelry box.

Rumors had spread that Chrissy had come to see Honey the night she went missing, and that Honey's father had done something to her. Honey had hated her father, but she didn't think he would have hurt Chrissy.

But this ribbon… What if her father *had* done something to Chrissy?

If so, why would he have kept the ribbon?

She'd never seen it before, and she'd used her jewelry box plenty of times after Chrissy went missing.

Maybe her father had hidden it, then after Honey moved out, he stashed it in the jewelry box, thinking that if anyone searched the premises and found it, they'd think it belonged to Honey.

Her hand trembled, the ribbon dangling between her fingers. If her father or Chrissy's abductor/killer had taken this ribbon, their fingerprints might be on it.

And she'd just contaminated it with her own.

Indecision warred in her mind. What should she do? She'd spent her childhood hiding her family's dirty little secrets. She could just stuff the ribbon back in the jewelry box and no one would ever know about it.

If she showed it to Harrison, he and everyone in town would assume, even believe, that her father was guilty of...murdering Chrissy.

Her stomach roiled. But could she keep quiet?

The Hawk family had been tormented for years, wondering what had happened to their little girl. They'd probably imagined a hundred different awful scenarios.

Although Mrs. Hawk hadn't liked Honey, Honey still had compassion for the woman and her family.

This ribbon might help them find the truth.

They deserved to have closure, didn't they?

HARRISON DREADED THE conversation with his family. Their dinners were meant to keep the family close, although Chrissy's disappearance had thrown a permanent kink in their relationships.

No dinner, holiday or amount of alcohol could smooth over the awkward tension between the brothers and their mother.

Still, he had to tell his family about Granger's death. Warn them that even if he didn't ask questions, others would.

Warn them that even though they might not have liked the man, it was Harrison's job to investigate his murder.

His phone buzzed just as he climbed inside his SUV. He checked the number. Honey Granger.

What did she want? Answers about her father's death?

Or maybe news about his body and what to do next?

The phone buzzed again, and he pressed Connect. "Sheriff Hawk."

Breathing rattled over the line. "Hello?"

"Harrison, it's me. Honey."

Her voice sounded shaky. Uncertain.

"Yes?"

"I…have to show you something. I don't know what it means or if it means anything, but, well, can you come out to my house? I mean, my father's house."

Harrison gritted his teeth. He had to deal with her, find her father's killer. But seeing her was difficult. It resurrected memories he'd tried to forget. And another kind of guilt—he should have stood up for Honey when his mother had judged her.

"Can you come?" Honey asked again.

"I'll be right there." Harrison's pulse clamored as he started the engine and drove toward the Granger's house. He phoned his deputy and asked him to do rounds around town.

Harrison had to be at his mother's house for dinner and drop the bombshell about Granger before she and his brothers heard the news from the local grapevine.

In a small town like Tumbleweed, word spread as quickly as butter melting on hot Texas pavement.

Night shadows hovered along the streets as he drove, the gray sky dark and desolate as he veered onto the road to Lower Tumbleweed. The yards were overgrown with weeds, the houses deserted, dilapidated and in need of repairs.

The neighborhood certainly didn't look welcoming or inviting to an outsider. The place probably held bad memories for Honey. An image of Honey, thin and wearing hand-me-downs two sizes too big for her, haunted him. She'd looked tiny and lost and lonely. She'd also been smart enough to understand the whispers and stares from the other kids.

No wonder she'd left town and never looked back.

He winced at the rotting porch with the brick for a makeshift step, then parked in the drive behind her van. Admiration for her for owning her own business mushroomed inside him. He didn't know how she'd done it, but he was proud of her for overcoming the obstacles her family had put in front of her. She'd made a success of herself in spite of adversity, an admirable accomplishment in his book.

He glanced around the unkempt yard and at the

peeling paint on the weathered house and wondered what Honey planned to do with the place. Sell it as it was or fix it up then sell? Judging from the lack of curb appeal and run-down condition of the homes, the comps would be low.

Curiosity over Honey's call nagged at him as he walked up to the front door. He raised his fist and knocked. A second later, she opened the door. Anxiety and some other emotion he couldn't quite define streaked her face.

Alarm bells clanged in his head. "Honey, is everything all right?"

She shook her head. "I don't know, Harrison. I... honestly don't know."

He forced his expression to remain professional. "Let me come in and then you can explain."

She chewed on her bottom lip, then stepped aside and motioned for him to enter. He scanned the living area. A mess. Granger had let everything go. Judging from the number of empty liquor and beer bottles, drinking had been his priority just as it had been when Honey lived here.

When she reached the sofa, she picked up what looked like a child's jewelry box, and ran her fingers over the rosewood design.

"What's wrong?" he asked quietly.

She took a deep breath, then gestured toward the jewelry box. "This... I was looking through things after I got home, trying to sort out my father's stuff and what was left of mine. I have to decide what to do with it all."

He nodded. "And?"

Misery darkened her eyes. "I found this." She pushed the jewelry box into his hands.

He narrowed his eyes, confused.

"Open it," she said tightly.

An uneasy feeling rolled through him. Whatever she'd found had upset her.

"Go ahead," she said. "I'm not sure what it means, but I had to show it to you."

He frowned, but slowly lifted the lid to the jewelry box. A slip of bright yellow caught his eyes.

A yellow ribbon. Just like the one his sister was wearing the night she disappeared.

"It was hers, wasn't it?" Honey asked in a choked voice.

He lifted his gaze to meet hers. The turmoil in her eyes mirrored how he felt at the moment. "It looks like Chrissy's. My brother said she was wearing yellow ones the night she disappeared."

"I know." Honey bit down on her lower lip.

"Did she come to your house that night?" Harrison asked.

Honey's hand trembled as she rubbed her temple. "If she did, I didn't see her," she said in a raw whisper.

"Don't lie to me, Honey. I know you wouldn't

have hurt Chrissy, but if you know something about your father…"

Tension escalated between them. "I don't. And if I did, I'd tell you. I want to know what happened to Chrissy, too."

The agony in her voice tore at him.

Of course the questions over Chrissy's disappearance had ripped her life inside and out, too.

"You really want the truth?" he asked gruffly.

She nodded. "We all deserve closure," she said softly.

That was one thing they agreed on.

"I'm sorry, but my fingerprints are on the ribbon," she said. "I wasn't thinking at first. But I'm sure you want to analyze it. If my dad's are there…"

Then that would mean that her father had touched the ribbon. That he'd either found it or taken it after he'd killed her.

He'd send it to the lab ASAP.

Two scenarios entered Harrison's mind. The first—Granger killed Chrissy and hid her body at the bluff. Then he'd returned to visit her.

But where had he hidden her? And why revisit her body now after all these years?

And if he had, who had killed him? Someone who'd discovered what he'd done?

Scenario two—Granger had been at the bluff and either stumbled on Chrissy's body or he stumbled on the killer, and the killer murdered him to keep him quiet.

HONEY COULD BARELY look at Harrison.

"Thank you for calling me, Honey," he said quietly. "I appreciate your honesty."

Honesty?

More guilt bombarded her. She hadn't mentioned that she'd been at the bluff that night, too. That if she'd been home, she'd know if Chrissy had come by. And she'd know if her father had done something to Chrissy or if he'd been passed out all evening.

His jaw tightened. "What if I find out that your father killed Chrissy?"

Honey sucked in a sharp breath. She and her father hadn't been close, but shame engulfed her. "Then we'll know."

The darkness in his eyes, a darkness filled with anger and pain, was a reminder that he and his family blamed her for his sister's disappearance.

If her father had killed Chrissy, he had a right to blame her.

Harrison shrugged. "The search parties never found anything belonging to my sister. Not her backpack or the pink jacket she was wearing or any clothing."

Honey thought back to the gossip after that night. "Some people thought that was a good sign. They thought she ran away and—"

"She didn't run away," Harrison said. "Chrissy may have argued with me and my brothers but she was afraid of the dark and wouldn't have gone out that night if Brayden hadn't convinced her to sneak out." He swallowed hard. "She was also attached to a stuffed doll that she won at a rodeo with my parents. She couldn't sleep without that rag doll." He paused, pain riddling his face. "If she was going to run away, she would have taken the doll."

Now that he mentioned it, Honey remembered the rag doll with the big blue painted eyes and red braided pigtails.

Honey had envied that doll because Chrissy had something Honey didn't—the innocence of childhood, which allowed her to play with dolls like a normal little girl.

Only Chrissy had lost her innocence—and maybe her life—that night.

"If you find any of those things, let me know."

"Of course," Honey said.

"Do you mind if I search the house?" Harrison asked.

Honey stiffened. "Go ahead. I'm not hiding anything."

His stormy gaze met hers, then he carried the ribbon to his SUV and returned with a flashlight.

Honey's phone buzzed just as he stepped back inside.

Her business partner, Jared.

She couldn't stand to watch Harrison comb through her father's house and her own personal childhood belongings, so she stepped outside to answer the phone.

"I have to take this," she said as he started to search her father's dresser drawers. She said a prayer he wouldn't find anything else belonging to Chrissy as she rushed outside to the front porch.

"How are things?" Jared asked.

"Not good." Honey bowed her head and fought the panic setting in.

"What happened?"

She hadn't shared her past with Jared, and she didn't want to now. "I just don't like being in my father's house."

He murmured that he understood. "When will you be back?"

A heaviness weighed on her. She'd felt trapped here as a teenager. She felt trapped now.

She couldn't leave until she had answers, until she knew who'd murdered her father.

Until she knew if he was a killer.

## Chapter Five

An hour later Harrison met Honey on the porch. "I'd like to come back during the day and look around the property."

Honey paled. "You think my father killed Chrissy and buried her here?"

Harrison shrugged. "I don't know what to think, Honey. But considering you found one of her ribbons, it's possible."

Honey clenched her hands together. She couldn't argue that point. "All right. Just let me know what time."

"I will." He studied her for another moment. He wanted to comfort her, but he had to do his job and it involved investigating her father. That was reality.

Just as reality meant that he had to talk to his family. Tonight.

For both their sakes, he hoped her father hadn't buried Chrissy on the Grangers' property.

He climbed into his SUV and cranked up the air as he drove toward the county lab. He dropped the ribbon off with instructions to send the results to his office ASAP.

Dark had set in as he drove through the entrance to Hawk's Landing. His father had first been drawn to the land because of the birds of prey that flocked to the south end. He claimed it was a sign that this land was meant to belong to him and that he was meant to build a family ranch on the property. He had insisted they keep a section as a natural habitat and sanctuary for the birds.

When he was a kid and needed time alone, Harrison used to ride his horse out to the corner of the property and watch the hawks soar. After Chrissy's disappearance, he'd found himself out there a lot.

His father had a huge wooden sign carved with the emblem of a hawk and had hung it over the gate to the ranch as a reminder of the birds.

Harrison checked his watch as he parked in the drive to his mother's Georgian home. He was half an hour late. His mother wouldn't be happy.

He wasn't happy, either.

Memories of playing on the property drifted back—fishing in the creek out back with his brothers, building the tree house with his father, playing horseshoes and baseball in the backyard.

So long ago.

All those fun times had ended abruptly when Chrissy disappeared. The house hadn't felt like a home but a tomb. The quiet had resounded with fear and grief. His mother had become a zombie. His father, angry all the time.

He'd shut down and his brothers had each retreated into their own rooms, silent and worried and alone.

Their vehicles were here now, though. When their father left, they'd formed an unspoken bond, knowing it was their job to take care of their mother. It hadn't been easy, but they'd survived.

Surviving was a long way from being whole, though.

Flowers filled the beds in front of the house, the roses climbing the trellis on the side a reminder that his mother loved gardening. It had become her therapy and filled her time.

He walked up the stone path to the door, his nerves on edge as he buzzed the doorbell. He didn't bother to wait for his mother to answer, though. He pushed open the door, slipped inside and removed his Stetson.

Voices sounded from the dining room, and he crossed the foyer, passed the living room and stepped into the dining room.

Lucas, Dexter and Brayden had gathered at the highboy, each with a drink in hand. Lucas had joined the FBI, Dexter had opened his own detective agency and Brayden was a lawyer.

He might need their help on the case. Maybe he could explain before he talked to their mother.

She bustled in a second later, her arms laden with food, and gave him a pointed look. "It's about time you got here."

"I'm sorry," he said, "it's been a busy day."

She set a plate of roast on the table, then mashed potatoes and gravy, and wiped her hands on her apron. "I guess it has. I heard you found Waylon Granger dead at the bluff."

Surprise made him stiffen. He glanced at his brothers but they looked at him stoically.

"Where did you hear that?" he asked.

"It doesn't matter," his mother said. "I'm just glad that man is dead."

THE QUESTIONS AND worry needling Honey made her feel restless and on edge. She stared at her father's house with a knot in her stomach.

Even exhausted, there was no way she could sleep right now.

She dug into the cabinet, grabbed some garbage bags and dived into cleaning out the closets. She started in her room and made two piles—one for trash and the other for donations to the local church.

There were very few toys, except for a few stuffed animals and a couple of dolls, so she dusted them off and placed them in the donation bag. The clothes she'd worn as a teenager were plain but someone might be able to use the jeans and flannel shirts. Everything else was either ragged or so frayed that she put them in the trash.

She stripped the gingham bedspread and sheets, then the ratty curtains, and stuffed them into the donation bag. Washed, they could be reused. But if she did anything with this house, she would gut it and stage it with new things to make it look more appealing.

When her room was bare, she moved to her father's room and did the same. His clothing was old and worn and reeked of smoke. Unable to salvage anything, she shoved everything into trash bags. Work boots, overalls, jeans, socks, underwear, shirts, belts—she didn't bother to even look at them. No one would want the outdated, threadbare items.

The faded chenille bedspread was marked with cigarette burns and stains, as were his sheets. She rolled the items up and added them to the trash.

She collected all the soda cans, liquor bottles and other trash and carried it to the garbage can outside. The refrigerator reeked of soured milk and several containers of molded food. She cleaned everything out, including the condiments, which had probably been in the fridge for ages.

Thankfully she found a bottle of cleaner beneath the sink so she wiped out the refrigerator and counters, then scrubbed the Formica table.

The small bathroom came next. Shaving cream, used soap and other toiletries went into the trash, along with the nasty shower curtain. If she sold the place, the bathroom would be gutted, too.

But if she was going to stay here until her father's murder was settled, she had to make the place livable. Even though the bathroom tiles and flooring were outdated, she scrubbed the toilet, sink, tub and walls until they smelled like cleaner.

Her shoulders and muscles ached as she piled the donation bags into her van. She pushed the garbage can to the curb for pickup, then piled the other trash bags beside it.

Tired but needing to get rid of the donation bags, she grabbed her purse and drove to town. She dropped the bags off first, then stopped by the discount store and stocked up on more cleaning supplies, a cheap shower curtain, sheets and a pillow for her bed. She added some scented candles to help alleviate the smoky smell, picked up a case of bottled water, coffee, cereal and milk for breakfast, then headed to the café for dinner.

An older couple had owned it when she lived here, but now it was named Cora's Café so it had changed owners. Did her former friend Cora own it now?

She was surprised to see that the place had been renovated. It still sported a Western theme, but the oak tables looked new, as did the sky blue curtains. Bar stools jutted up to a counter for extra seating, and country music echoed through the room, a backdrop to the chatter and laughter. A chalkboard showcased a handwritten menu with the specials for the day.

Customers filled the booths and tables, evidenced by the number of cars outside. The scent of fried chicken and apple pie made her stomach growl.

A woman about her age with auburn hair in a pixie cut greeted her. "Honey, I heard you were back in town. I'm sorry about your father."

She smiled, grateful to see her old friend "Hi, Cora. I was thinking about you today. So you own the café now?"

Cora handed her a menu. "I bought it a couple of years ago and did a makeover. Guess cooking for the family all those years paid off."

"It looks good."

"Thanks." Cora blushed, and Honey smiled, grateful she seemed happy.

She noticed a booth to the far right and started toward it. Suddenly the room grew quiet, though, and an uneasy feeling prickled her spine.

She glanced around and noted several people looking at her.

She'd forgotten what it was like to live in a small town. Everyone knew everyone else. When a stranger visited, everyone knew that, too.

She offered them a tentative smile, but memories of being the hub of gossip made her want to run.


HARRISON GRITTED HIS teeth at the questioning looks from his brothers and his mother. Maybe he should have called and given them a heads-up.

"You didn't think to tell us before everyone in town knew?" Dexter asked.

Harrison took a deep breath before he responded. "I came here as soon as I could. I don't know how word leaked. It shouldn't have."

"Well, it did." His mother pushed her bangs off her forehead with a smile. The fact that the hair found at the crime scene was short and brown didn't escape him. His mother's hair was short and brown.

Lucas lifted his drink glass in a gesture of offering. "Fix you one and then we'll toast."

"What are we toasting?" Harrison asked gruffly.

"That Waylon Granger is dead," his mother said. "Tumbleweed is better off without him."

Harrison's patience was wearing thin. It had been a long damn day. "How can you say that, Mother? Granger was a crappy father, but we don't have proof he did anything else." Honey's face flashed in his mind. *She* didn't deserve any of this.

His mother patted his shoulder. "You always were the diplomat, Harrison. But we know, at least *I* know, that that damned man hurt our Chrissy."

Harrison glanced at his brothers to see if they were in agreement. Lucas sipped his drink, his expression neutral. Dexter slipped an arm around their mother as if to offer support. Brayden poured himself another drink, then fixed Harrison one and offered it to him.

Harrison took it, struggling to think of a way to defuse the situation. And how to subtly ask his family when they'd last seen Granger.

He sipped the whiskey, grateful for the warmth sliding down his throat. "Do any of you have evidence to prove that Granger did something to our sister?"

"Not yet," Lucas said.

Dexter cleared his throat. "I talked to Waylon's neighbors but no one remembered seeing Chrissy that night. They couldn't say he was at home all night, either."

"When did you talk to them?" Harrison asked.

"As soon as I got my PI license. But three of the families who lived in that neighborhood had already moved."

Brayden's look turned dark. "Have you found anything to incriminate him?"

Harrison bit his tongue. He didn't want to reveal what he'd found or learned; not yet. People would convict Granger—and he wanted the truth, not a vigilante situation.

But his family deserved answers.

"Let's sit down and eat before dinner gets cold." His mother ushered them to their usual chairs and for a few minutes, the discussion was put on hold as they served themselves from the platters of roast beef, potatoes and gravy and green beans.

Although Harrison wanted to gulp down his whiskey, he forced himself to eat instead. He still had work to do.

"How did Granger die?" Dexter asked as he forked up a bite of roast.

Harrison studied his family, searching for any sign that one of them already knew the truth. Emotions strained everyone's faces, as if just mentioning Granger's name stirred up the horrid memories of the night Chrissy disappeared.

His mother had been near hysterical when she

and his father arrived home from their party and discovered Brayden and Chrissy weren't home.

Harrison had felt sick to his stomach—it was his fault they'd sneaked out. His fault they'd been at the bluff because they'd followed him.

Brayden had raced in on his bike with his ankle swollen, ready to fuss at Chrissy for not sending help, then realized she hadn't made it back to their house. Fear had ignited tempers, and a lot of screaming and yelling had ensued.

His parents had frantically called Chrissy's best friends but both of them had been home in bed and hadn't seen or talked to Chrissy.

His mother dropped her fork with a clatter. "What aren't you telling us, Harrison?"

His brothers stopped chewing and stared at him as if they, too, realized there was more to the story. Damn.

Harrison took another swig of his whiskey. "Granger didn't die of natural causes."

"What?" His mother gasped.

His brothers gave him questioning looks. "What's going on?" Dexter asked.

Harrison swallowed hard. "He was murdered."

His mother clamped her teeth over her bottom lip, then lifted her glass of wine. "Well, he got what he deserved."

Harrison agreed with her. But he still had to find out who killed the man. A silent prayer formed on his lips that his family had nothing to do with it.

HONEY SLIPPED INTO a booth, hoping to avoid attention. A teenager wearing tattered jeans and a denim shirt appeared, an order pad in her hands. Black square glasses framed a thin, pale face. A sadness radiated from the girl as if she had problems bigger than a teenager should.

Honey felt a kinship with her. At fifteen she'd worked at the Dairy Barn to make money so she could leave town. Did this girl have problems like she'd had? Did she have any family who cared about her?

Had Cora hired her because she wanted to help?

"What can I get you?"

Her name tag read Sonya. "A turkey sandwich and a bowl of that vegetable soup."

"Sure. What do you want to drink?"

Wine would be nice but the diner didn't serve it. "Just water. Oh, and a cup of coffee. Decaf, please." She didn't need caffeine to keep her awake tonight. It would be hard enough to sleep in her father's house anyway.

The girl nodded then made her way to the counter and dropped off Honey's order. She returned a minute later with the coffee and water.

Honey stirred sugar into her mug then sipped it, her gaze scanning the room. Two older couples sat having coffee and pie while a group of teens chowed on burgers and fries at a table near the door.

Three gray-haired women were huddled around a table beside her sipping tea.

"Did you hear that Waylon Granger died at the bluff?" the curly-haired woman with glasses said.

The other two women's faces expressed surprise.

The thin lady in a blue knit pantsuit leaned over the table, eyes wide. "Really?"

The curly-haired woman clinked her spoon on her teacup. "He sure did. My grandson was up there and found him. Waylon fell over that ridge."

The third lady clacked her teeth. "Wonder what he was doing up there?"

"Probably drunk," the thin lady said.

"He was always drunk," the curly-haired one whispered. "Such a sorry excuse for a man."

The third lady pushed her pie plate away, the pie half-eaten. "You know the Hawks always thought he killed their little girl, Chrissy?"

Honey averted her face so she didn't have to look at the women, but their voices reached her anyway.

"I heard that, too," the curly-haired one said. "He did have a temper."

"He sure did. I always felt sorry for that girl of his. No wonder she left town."

"I thought she left because she was pregnant."

"Could have been."

Honey sank down in the booth, hoping no one recognized her.

"I figured the Hawks ran her off," the woman continued. "I heard Ava saying that Granger's girl was white trash."

"If you ask me, Ava shouldn't have been pointing a finger."

"What do you mean?"

"Well, the night their little girl went missing, the Hawks were at a party for the mayor." She paused dramatically. "Steven accused Ava of having an affair."

The other women gasped. "What?"

"No."

"They were talking about Chrissy, too. Made me think that she wasn't Steven's baby."

"What did Ava say?"

"I don't know. They left in a huff."

Honey tensed. She despised gossip because she'd borne the brunt of it.

But what if the Hawks' marriage hadn't been perfect like everyone thought? What if Ava Hawk had had an affair?

What if Chrissy wasn't Steven Hawk's child?

# Chapter Six

Honey's head reeled. Harrison's father had left the family and town a few months after the investigation into Chrissy's disappearance went cold.

Rumors surfaced then that he had something to do with his daughter's disappearance. Others whispered that he'd left because the tragedy of losing his daughter had broken his heart.

She drummed her fingers on the table. Now she wondered—had he left because his wife had cheated on him?

The waitress appeared with her soup and sandwich, and Honey thanked her, then dug in. She hadn't realized she was so hungry but hadn't eaten since breakfast and was starved.

The women stood, gathering their purses and hats, and Honey sank lower in the booth, angling her face away from them in case they recognized her. The woman in the blue knit pantsuit paused and peered at her, but Honey looked down at her phone to avoid eye contact.

The bell on the door tinkled as it opened and they left, then a tall woman with sharp features entered, a big guy with an awkward gait beside her holding her hand. One of his eyes looked blurry, his mouth twitched and he made an odd, high-pitched sound.

"Let's sit in that booth, Elden," the woman said.

Honey straightened. Elden?

She'd known him. Elden Lynch was three years older than she was and mentally challenged. She'd felt sorry for him because the kids at school made fun of him. Worse, some of the parents had been afraid of him and had warned their children away from him. Not that he was mean or violent.

In fact, he was sweet and childlike and just wanted to make friends.

He shuffled past, rocking his head back and forth. It was him, the boy she'd known.

Honey was tempted to say something, but his mother glared at her.

Mrs. Lynch ushered him into a chair. "Stay put, Elden."

The big woman stepped over to Honey's booth. "I heard you were back in town."

Honey tensed at the vehemence in her tone.

"I don't know if you're staying around here," Mrs. Lynch continued, "but if you are, keep away from my son. He doesn't need any trouble."

"I'm not here to cause trouble," Honey said, her voice firm. "I—"

"Then get your sorry daddy buried and leave town," Mrs. Lynch barked. "Tumbleweed is better off without any of you Grangers."

Hurt and anger bled through Honey. She wanted to defend her father and herself.

But an image of that yellow ribbon taunted her, and she kept her mouth shut.

When word about that surfaced, people would definitely condemn her father.

It shouldn't bother her. He had been a sorry drunk.

Elden's mother didn't have to worry about her staying. She'd leave as soon as possible.

"MOTHER," HARRISON SAID, measuring his words carefully, "I wouldn't go around telling everyone how glad you are that Waylon Granger is dead."

She gave him a sharp look. "Why not? I am glad he's dead."

"He was murdered," Harrison said, hoping to drive home his point. "That means there has to be an investigation."

Brayden's lawyer instincts quickly kicked in. "He's warning you not to incriminate yourself, Mother."

She finished her wine then set the glass on the table with an eyebrow raise. "And you're the sheriff so you're going to find out who killed him?"

Harrison nodded. "That's the way it works."

"How was he murdered?" Dexter asked.

Harrison wiped his mouth with his napkin. "I don't have an official statement from the ME, but it appears he was struck on the back of the head with a rock, then pushed over the edge of the ridge."

Other than his mother's eyes widening slightly, she showed no reaction.

"You find any forensics?" Lucas asked.

Harrison maintained a neutral expression. "I found a rock that might be the one that struck him. It's at the lab now, being tested."

"Anything else?" Brayden asked.

"CSI found a button in the bushes and a short brown hair that was caught on Granger."

"The teenagers still go up there," his mother said, ignoring the comment about the brown hair. "That button could be one of theirs."

Harrison narrowed his eyes. Was his mother trying to cover for herself? "True. But it was close to the ledge, so we'll test it for prints."

She tore a roll in half and buttered it.

"Mother, where were you last night?"

Brayden laid his hand over their mother's. "You don't have to answer that."

"Are you asking as my son or as the sheriff?" his mother said quietly.

Emotions clogged Harrison's throat at the hurt in his mother's voice. Her screams the night Chrissy went missing echoed in his head, resurrecting guilt and anguish.

How could he interrogate his own mother after what he'd put her through?

She squeezed Brayden's hand. "It's all right, Brayden. Actually I don't mind answering. I was home all night."

Brayden's eyes went dark. "Was anyone here with you, Mother? Anyone who can corroborate your story?"

She stiffened. "It's not a story, it's the truth. And no one was here. I had one of my migraines so I took a pill and went to bed early."

"How about phone calls?" Harrison asked.

She sighed. "Like I said, I took a pill and went to bed early. If the phone rang, I didn't hear it."

Harrison raked a hand through his hair. Dammit, he wanted her to have a rock-solid alibi.

"I'm not the only one who disliked Waylon Granger," his mother said.

"But no one else had a motive to kill him," Harrison pointed out.

"Harrison," Lucas cut in, his voice hard. "You're not accusing Mom of murder, are you?"

Harrison folded his arms. "No, but it's my job to ask questions and find out the truth."

"The truth is that the town is better off without that lowlife in it," his mother said curtly.

"We have no proof that he hurt anyone," Harrison said, testing the waters to see if one of his family members mentioned the ribbon.

"He hurt his own daughter," Dexter said. "Everyone in Tumbleweed knew that but no one did anything to help her."

Dexter was right. *Someone* should have stepped in and protected Honey.

"That girl wasn't worth saving," his mother said. "She was white trash just like her mama."

"She was only a kid." A trace of bitterness laced his voice. "She never did anything wrong."

"My God, you're defending her." His mother gave him a lethal look. "She probably lied about that night, Harrison. Chrissy always tried to sneak over and see that girl. I bet she did that night but Honey lied to protect her old man."

Harrison tossed his napkin on the table. "You were always unfair to her, Mother. And for your information, Honey hasn't held anything back. She hasn't defended her father or pointed the finger at anyone over his death." In fact, she'd given Harrison the ribbon she'd found at her father's house.

But he refused to share that information. His mother would convict Granger and Honey without any further questions.

His mother's hand slapped the table. "Oh, my God, she's back, isn't she?"

Harrison heaved a breath. "Yes, I had to inform her of her father's death."

"So you've seen her?" his mother asked, her disappointment palpable.

"Yes," Harrison said through gritted teeth. "At the morgue."

His mother frowned. "She's not going to stay around, is she?"

"I doubt it," Harrison said. Why would she want to? The people in Tumbleweed had been brutal to her. "But she has to bury her father."

"The next time you see her, make her tell you what he did with Chrissy," his mother said.

Disgust ate at Harrison. He'd felt sorry for his

mother after Chrissy went missing and had blamed himself. He'd wanted to see her happy again.

But he didn't like her much at the moment.

He shoved away from the table. "Thanks for dinner, but I have to go."

"Ask her," his mother yelled as he stalked from the room. "Make her tell you, Harrison!"

He slammed the front door as he left. The sound of his mother's harsh, accusatory voice reverberated in his head, though, as he made it to his SUV.

THAT SAME SICK feeling she'd had years ago twisted Honey's stomach. She hadn't lived in Tumbleweed in nearly two decades, but Mrs. Lynch still remembered her and hated her.

Just because she'd been born on the wrong side of the tracks.

The young waitress stepped up to the Lynches' table. "Hey, Elden," the girl said sweetly. "How are you?"

Mrs. Lynch pulled her son closer to her as she glared at the waitress. "He's fine. Just take our order and leave us alone."

"Of course," the waitress said with a pained look. "What would you like?"

Elden made that odd sound again, then his mother ordered for both of them and the waitress disappeared.

Honey had little tolerance for bullies and judgmental people who discriminated against those different than themselves, whether it was race, ethnicity, gender, disabilities or social status.

Agitated, she finished her meal and paid the bill.

No use making a scene and drawing more attention to herself. She didn't intend to stay in this Podunk place and fight a battle she'd lost years ago.

She doubled the waitress's tip, then hurried outside to her van. The hair on the back of her neck prickled as she climbed in the driver's side. Was someone watching her?

She scanned the parking lot. Several teens were hanging out around a black pickup. Two older men huddled near the back door, heads bent, smoke curling from their cigarettes. A motor rumbled from somewhere in the parking lot. A horn honked. Directly across from her, a dark sedan with tinted windows was parked. Its lights flickered on, nearly blinding her.

Anxious to leave, she started the van, her pulse pounding when she pulled onto the road. The dark sedan followed. She wove through town, making several turns, hoping to lose the car, but it stayed behind her.

Heart drumming, she sped up and drove toward the sheriff's office. She slowed as she approached it. The sedan was still behind her.

Nerves on edge, she jerked her vehicle into the parking lot in front of the sheriff's office.

The sedan slowed and coasted by her. She tried

to see the driver inside, but it was too dark outside and his windows were practically black.

The car finally went on, and she leaned her head into her hands and inhaled several deep breaths. She checked the parking lot for Harrison's police SUV. If he was inside, she'd tell him about the car.

But what could he do now? The sedan had already gone. And what if the driver hadn't been following her?

Why would anyone follow her anyway? No one but Harrison knew she was in town; well, except for Mrs. Lynch and the people who'd seen her at the café. But why would one of them want to scare her?

Shaking her head at herself for being paranoid, she pulled back onto the road and drove to Lower Tumbleweed. Her shoulders and muscles ached from fatigue and the stress of the day as she parked at her father's house.

The streetlights in the neighborhood had long ago burned out, casting an eerie darkness to the houses and overgrown properties.

Tomorrow she'd talk to her father's lawyer and finish cleaning out this place. Hell, if she had to, she could hire a crew to come in and empty it out.

So far, there was nothing she'd found inside that she wanted to keep.

Just as she climbed from the van and headed up the walkway to the porch, car lights flickered. She glanced back at the road, her pulse spiking.

That dark sedan was driving by her house.

Her hand trembled as she shoved the key into the lock. She fumbled with it, dropped the keys then picked them up. The sedan slowed, almost pausing in front of the house as if the driver was stalking her.

She jammed the key into the lock, twisted it and shoved the door open. The telephone inside was ringing as she fell into the foyer and slammed the door closed. She twisted the lock frantically and looked out the window. The sedan was still there.

The phone trilled again.

Nerves rattled, she darted to the table for her phone. Maybe it was Harrison calling to check on her. Praying it was so, she clenched the handset.

"Hello," she said shakily.

Heavy breathing rattled over the line.

She ran to the window and looked outside, the phone still in her hand.

More breathing.

Anger rallied inside her, blending with fear. "Who is this?"

Another heavy breath. Then a low, throaty voice. "Get out of Tumbleweed or you'll end up like your father."

# *Chapter Seven*

"Harrison, wait up!"

Harrison paused by his car. He'd had to leave or he would have lost his temper with his mother.

Footsteps crunched gravel, the air charged as Lucas and Dexter joined him.

Harrison braced himself for a confrontation. "I know Mom's upset—"

"Brayden is trying to calm her down," Dexter said.

"Good. She may need a lawyer." He prayed it didn't come to that, but his cop instincts screamed that it might.

Lucas stared at him head-on. He was the same height as Harrison and they had similar builds. But even as the younger brother, Lucas could be intimidating. "What aren't you telling us?" Lucas asked.

"Yeah, spill it, brother," Dexter added. "We might be able to help."

Harrison clenched his jaw. That was true. Lucas was FBI and Dexter, a PI. "I told you all I know."

"Come on," Dexter said. "You're not talking to Mom. It's us."

"Yeah, we have as much interest in Granger as you do," Lucas said.

He doubted that. "I'm the one who was supposed to babysit that night," Harrison said gruffly. "It was my fault we lost our sister, and it's my job to find out what happened to her."

Dexter cursed. "Your fault? Hell, it was mine. I got mad at Chrissy that night because she kept following me around and I told her to get lost." His voice cracked. "Then she did."

Harrison studied Dexter with new eyes. He hadn't realized Dexter harbored guilt as he did.

"It's not either of your faults," Lucas said. "But it might be mine."

Harrison and Dexter both frowned at Lucas. "What are you talking about?" Harrison asked.

Lucas looked tortured as he glanced back at their childhood home. "I should have said something a long time ago."

Dexter cleared his throat. "About what?"

Lucas heaved a weary breath. "I was a jerk to Chrissy back then. You remember Geoffrey Williams?"

"He was that cool kid whose family had all that money, wasn't he?" Dexter said.

"He's on the town council now," Harrison said.

Lucas nodded. "He was the captain of the baseball team. I thought if I sucked up to him, he'd tell the coach to let me be assistant captain."

"What does this have to do with Chrissy?" Harrison asked.

Lucas rubbed the back of his neck. "Chrissy wanted to tag along with us to the fields, but Geoffrey didn't want a kid around. He told her to leave us alone, then he pushed her down. I...just stood there. I didn't do anything to defend her."

"You all were just kids," Dexter said.

Lucas shrugged. "Maybe. But later I realized how mean Geoffrey was. I saw him push some other little girl around, too. He was a bully. It made me wonder if he might have done something to Chrissy."

Harrison considered the information. "Was Geoffrey at the bluff that night?"

Lucas nodded. "Yes, I ran into him while we were out searching for Chrissy."

"Did you see him with Chrissy?" Dexter asked.

Lucas shook his head. "No. But he had dirt on his jacket. He said he skidded on the hill by the cave but...later, I wondered if he might have seen Chrissy. He could have shoved her again and she could have fallen over the edge or maybe he saw her in the cave..."

Harrison had no idea that Lucas blamed himself all these years or that he'd had his own theory about what happened to Chrissy.

"Why didn't you tell someone about this back then?" Dexter said.

Guilt and anguish darkened Lucas's eyes.

"Because you still wanted him to name you assistant captain," Harrison finished.

Lucas nodded. "I should have spoken up, said something."

Harrison and Dexter exchanged worried looks. "You're right. I can use the help. Talk to Williams."

Lucas shifted. "All right, I will."

"What can I do?" Dexter asked.

"Track down and question all of the kids who were at the bluff that night. Maybe someone lied or remembers something and is ready to talk."

Harrison's cell phone buzzed at his hip. He jerked it up and checked the caller ID. Honey Granger.

Aware his brothers were watching and listening, he answered the way he did on a business call. "Sheriff Hawk."

"Harrison, it's Honey." Her voice warbled. "Someone just called and threatened me."

Harrison tensed. "Are you all right?"

"Yes," Honey said. "But I'm scared."

Harrison cursed. "I'll be right there."

HONEY'S HAND TREMBLED as she ended the call. She rushed back to the window and peeked out. The sedan screeched away, disappearing into the night and leaving her with the eerie sensation that the threatening call had come from whoever was in that car.

She tried to read the license plate, but it was too dark.

Nerves raw, she clenched her phone and ran through the house to make sure no one was inside.

The rooms looked disheveled from her cleaning rampage, but nothing appeared to be missing and no one was inside.

Satisfied an intruder wasn't hiding in the house,

she hurried back to the living room to wait for Harrison. Too antsy to sit or relax, she yanked another trash bag from the box and filled it with old magazines to take to recycling.

Several minutes later the sound of a motor rumbling startled her, and she rushed to the window. Harrison.

Relief filled her, and she opened the door and met him on the porch.

Harrison's dark gaze raked over her, concern in his eyes. "Are you all right?"

She nodded although tears pricked her eyes. She'd told herself she had to be strong and not lean on anyone, but she couldn't help herself. She threw herself against him and dropped her head forward, her breathing erratic.

He felt so big and strong, solid as a rock. A comfort in the wake of the night's unsettling events.

For a brief second his body tensed, muscles bunching, his breath puffing against her hair. But then he wrapped his arms around her and stroked her back.

"It's going to be okay, Honey," he murmured. "I'll make things right."

She leaned into him and closed her eyes. She wanted to believe him, but no one could change the past or make people think differently of her.

As soon as he murmured the promise, Harrison regretted it. Remembering his mother's reaction to

Granger's death stirred fear that she had something to do with his murder.

But why would she have killed him now, after all the time that had passed?

Had she learned something incriminating against him then confronted him?

Honey's fingers dug into his chest, and he held her tighter, hating the fact that someone had frightened her.

Worse, what if his mother had called her to scare her off? She'd made no bones about the fact that she disliked Honey and didn't want her in Tumbleweed.

He rubbed Honey's back, his fingers brushing the long, silky strands of her golden hair. She felt small and fragile and so damn feminine that Harrison's body hardened in response.

He closed his eyes, hoping to rein in his libido. But she shifted against him, her belly brushed his sex and heat rippled through him.

His sex pulsed, thick and aching, and need hit him hard.

Dammit. It had been a long time since a woman had aroused him like this.

And Honey Granger was the last woman on earth he wanted to feel this way about. But she was vulnerable and had been hurt by his family and this town, and protective instincts surged through him.

Just as his brother felt bad for not standing up for Chrissy, he regretted not defending Honey years ago.

He wasn't an impressionable kid anymore. He would stand up for her this time if she needed it.

HE SLOWLY PULLED back until their bodies were no longer touching. He had to before he did something insane like kiss her or slide his hand lower to feel the curve of her breast or even lower to her hip.

He moved his hands to her arms and held her facing him. "Tell me exactly what happened."

She pushed a strand of hair from her face and blinked, then seemed to compose herself. "I dropped some of Dad's old clothes at the church, then stopped at the café to get something to eat." She hesitated as if debating what to say.

"Go on," Harrison said.

"I saw a guy there, Elden Lynch, who I remembered from childhood."

"I know Elden," Harrison said. "He was mentally disabled from birth, but he's harmless."

"I know. I was friendly to him when we were kids, but tonight his mother told me to leave him alone."

Harrison clenched his jaw again. "Mrs. Lynch is not always nice. She's very protective of her son."

Honey shrugged. "I guess I can't blame her. He was bullied terribly when he was young."

"People still stare at him and whisper behind his back," Harrison said grimly.

"Some things never change," Honey said.

Harrison nodded, although he didn't like it. "What happened next?"

Honey rubbed her arms in a nervous gesture. "I saw a dark sedan in the parking lot and it followed me."

"Did you see the driver?"

"No, it was dark and the windows were tinted." That figured.

"I pulled up to your office to see if I could lose him and he went on," Honey continued. "But when I got home, the same car showed up in the street. I ran inside and locked the door, and it stopped in front of the house. That's when my phone rang."

"You think the person in the car was the caller?"

Honey nodded. "I don't know, maybe."

"What exactly did the caller say?"

"He said, 'Get out of Tumbleweed or you'll end up like your father.'"

Harrison sucked in a breath. "The voice was male?"

Honey's brow furrowed. "I'm not sure. It was low, muffled. It could have been a woman."

They were getting nowhere. "Did he—or she—say anything else?"

Honey shook her head. "I asked who it was, but the phone went dead."

"Did the call come in on your cell phone?"

"No, the landline in the house."

So the caller phoned Granger's house. "That

could be good news. He or she doesn't have your cell phone."

"But whoever it is knows I'm staying here."

"True." And he didn't like that one little bit. "I'll stay here tonight to make sure you're safe," Harrison said.

Panic flashed in Honey's eyes. "No, I couldn't ask you to do that."

Harrison patted his badge. "I'm the sheriff, Honey. It's my job to protect the citizens and anyone visiting Tumbleweed."

"I am just visiting," Honey said.

"I figured as much."

"Although maybe I should leave town," Honey said. "I could hire someone to clear out the rest of my father's house."

"You could." For some reason, he didn't want Honey to leave. Not yet.

Honey straightened, lifting her chin. "No, I'm not going to let anyone run me off. Not ever again."

"Like you did when you were eighteen?"

Honey's gaze met his, emotions brimming in her beautiful eyes. Eyes that had seen pain and heartache. Eyes that flared with a determination that he admired.

"I want to know the truth about who killed my father and if he hurt Chrissy."

So did he. But they might not like the answers they found.

Still, he'd become sheriff to find justice for Chrissy. And nothing would stop him.

## Chapter Eight

Harrison didn't like the fact that someone had threatened Honey. Granted, the call could be a prank or a meaningless threat, but her father had just been murdered and she was staying in the man's house.

Maybe whoever killed him was afraid Honey would find something inside the house or on the property.

"Thank you for offering to stay," Honey said. "But I'll be fine, Harrison. I'm accustomed to staying alone."

Did that mean she wasn't involved with anyone?

"I don't feel good about leaving you," Harrison admitted.

Honey lifted her chin. "Don't worry. I have protection."

He arched a brow. "You have a gun?"

She nodded. "I carry it when I look at properties. Sometimes I go into bad areas, and there've been a few times when someone was squatting inside one of the abandoned houses I was looking at to purchase."

Harrison crossed his arms. "So you know how to use the gun?"

"Yes." A look of defiance streaked her eyes. "I've been on my own since I left Tumbleweed."

He'd wondered about that. "You didn't go to live with other family?"

"I have no other family," Honey said.

Curiosity ate at Harrison. She had only been eighteen, a kid when she'd left. "How did you survive?"

Honey averted her eyes as if to avoid eye contact. "It's not important, Harrison. What's important is that I can take care of myself."

Only she'd been terrified and shaking earlier.

She didn't like being vulnerable, though; that was obvious. And she didn't want to need him or his help.

But she did need it.

"All right, but call me if you receive another threat or if that sedan shows up. I'll have my deputy check around to see if anyone in town drives a car like that."

She nodded and stepped back toward the door. "Thanks for coming out."

"That's my job," Harrison said, although even if he wasn't sheriff and he thought she was in danger, he would have driven over. No woman should have to be afraid in her own house.

"Right."

Her curt tone made him tense and reminded him that she and his family had been on opposite sides for years. That Honey had reason to dislike him and the Hawks.

"I'll be back in the morning with a warrant to search the property."

His comment brought pain back to her eyes, but also resignation.

He moved onto the brick step, scanning the yard and sides for trouble as he strode to his SUV. When he climbed inside, he glanced back at the shabby house and saw Honey at the window, watching him.

The idea of her alone at eighteen made his stomach knot. The idea of someone threatening her and possibly following through made that knot tighten even more.

She closed the blinds, and he pictured her undressing, slipping into pajamas and retrieving her gun to sleep with.

The image aroused him and stirred admiration for her independence.

It also made him want to go inside, crawl into bed and tell her she didn't need a gun, that he would take care of her.

Shaken by that thought, he started the engine. He phoned his deputy and asked him to check the databases to see if anyone in town owned a dark sedan. As he expected, a dozen or more popped up.

Geoffrey Williams was one. But, hell, so were the mayor and Cora Zimmerman and the local preacher.

Still, he spent the next hour driving from Honey's house to town and back, searching for the sedan.

No one would hurt Honey, not as long as he was sheriff.

HONEY LAY AWAKE for hours in her childhood bed, torn by memories of growing up.

As a child, she always locked her bedroom door.

Tonight she left it ajar so she could hear if an intruder broke in.

The day took its toll, though, and she finally fell into an exhausted sleep. Dreams of hiding in the closet when her father was in a drunken rage mixed with nightmares of showing up at school in mismatched, raggedy clothes and running from the mean girls who'd laughed at her and called her names.

She wanted to join in and had inched up to the circle of girls at the edge of the bleachers. But one of them spotted her and started laughing.

"Go away," one of the girls yelled. "We don't want you around."

She turned and ran. They chased her onto the football field where she fell face-first in a mud puddle. She pushed herself up, face and clothes covered in mud, and tried to stand, but she slipped and hit the wet ground again.

When she looked up through tear-soaked eyes, the football team was laughing. Harrison was standing at the edge of the field, stone-faced and disapproving as if she'd interrupted their game.

She scrambled up and ran from the field toward the woods. She wanted to get lost. Never go back again.

But where would she go? She was underage, would have to live on the streets. Her house was dangerous, but she wasn't stupid.

The streets would be worse.

Still she ran into the woods. At least she could hide there until school was out. Then she'd run home and clean up the mud.

She tripped over a tree stump and hit the ground. Weeds clawed at her hands and she tasted dirt.

A NOISE SUDDENLY jarred her awake. Honey clenched the sheets and sat up to search the room. Cool air brushed her cheek, and she jerked her head to the side. The window was busted.

Moonlight shone in, illuminating a rock on the floor.

Another loud sound, glass shattering. She slid from bed, grabbed her robe and pulled it on, then slid her gun from the nightstand. Gripping it with both hands, she tiptoed to the bedroom door and looked around the living room and kitchen.

She didn't see anyone, but she went still and listened. The floor creaked. The wind whistled. The sheers in the living room billowed out as the wind blew through the shattered window.

Was someone inside?

Tense seconds dragged by. More glass breaking. The second window in the living room. Then another crash—the window in the kitchen.

The rock hit the floor, glass spraying.

She startled and bit back a gasp.

Someone was throwing rocks at her house. Why? To scare her off?

She inched toward the window and peered out but she didn't see anyone. The sound came again, this time from her father's room, then her room.

Someone was breaking all the windows. Was it the person who'd threatened her earlier?

She inched back toward the bedroom and grabbed her phone. She hated to call Harrison a second time in one night, but she was scared.

What if this was the same person who'd killed her father?

Another noise made her jerk her head toward the back door. She held her breath, straining to hear as she crept through the hall. Another loud noise. The rock hitting the door.

Heart racing, she punched Harrison's number.

HARRISON HAD JUST dozed off when the phone jarred him awake. He snatched it on the second ring.

"Harrison, it's Honey. I'm sorry to bother you but someone is throwing rocks through my windows."

What the hell? His feet hit the floor and he was dressed in seconds. "Lock the door and stay inside. I'll be right there."

He flipped his siren on as he got in his SUV, senses alert as he sped toward Lower Tumbleweed. The road was deserted, most houses dark, the citizens of Tumbleweed safely tucked in for the night.

Except for Honey.

Who the hell would throw rocks at her house this time of the night—or morning?

Dawn streaked the sky, the morning sun struggling to peek through the dark clouds. Dust blurred the horizon as the wind swept it from the abandoned farm. Desperate for rain, the grass was turning brown and the crops were hurting from thirst.

Deciding he didn't want to alert the culprit at Honey's with his siren, he flipped it off and slowed, cruising slowly down the street and searching for signs of trouble. The houses neighboring Honey's father's house were vacant, the run-down properties desolate and forgotten.

He should have stayed here tonight as he'd suggested to Honey.

What if she was hurt?

Images of her bloody and unconscious flashed behind his eyes. Then an image of her lying dead like her father.

If whoever had killed her father thought something in the house might incriminate him, he might try to frighten her off with a warning—or come after her.

He scanned both sides of the road and the woods backing up to the houses, but didn't see a car or a person. But the houses on both sides of Honey's had shattered windows, the panes broken out.

He cut his lights and veered into the Grangers' driveway. The lights in the den were on. The blinds slid open and Honey peered at him. Relief flooded her face.

He paused to listen for sounds of the culprit, but the whistling of the wind rattling the leaves on the trees was the only sound in the night.

He motioned to Honey that he was going to check the property, and she gave a nod. He pulled his flashlight from his pocket and shone it to the right of the house in search of the perp. Nothing but trees and a cat that darted from behind the neighboring house.

He flicked it across the front of the house. Both front windows were shattered. Turning in a wide arc, he scanned the ground for footprints. The grass looked marred, flattened in places from foot impressions.

But the rocks and dirt blended with the grass and he couldn't determine a definitive print. A partial near the sidewalk indicated the foot had been large, but he couldn't discern if the shoe was a sneaker or boot.

Damn.

He walked around the side of the house, searching the ground for more footprints or something the perp might have dropped. The side window had also been shattered. When he reached the back door, he spotted indentations in the wood from the impact of the rock. More than once. Wood had splintered to the point that the rotting board had a hole in it.

Anger surged through Harrison.

Honey hadn't done anything to deserve this.

He strode toward the woods, grass, leaves and brush crunching beneath his boots. A twig snapped. The sound of a coyote howled in the distance.

He spotted movement in the woods and shone his flashlight in the direction where he'd seen it. Seconds dragged by as he searched. Finally another movement deep in the woods.

An animal or the predator who'd terrorized Honey?

It was too damn far away to tell.

He glanced back at the house, tempted to give chase, but what if he was wrong and the movement was a damn deer and he left Honey alone and vulnerable?

Cursing again, he continued walking the back of the property, then veered left to the other side of the house. Another window shattered, this one in the laundry room.

No wonder Honey had been frightened. She'd been attacked from all sides. Had there been more than one perpetrator?

He shone the light toward the land connecting to the Grangers' place. The house was deserted and falling in. Rotting boards sagged on the exterior. The windows had also been shattered.

Irritated and worried about Honey, he conducted one more sweep of the property, circling the house. He stepped onto the makeshift step then jumped onto the porch.

Honey opened the door before he could even knock.

He swept his gaze over her, needing to know that she was okay. Safe. Unhurt.

"I'm sorry I called," she said, "but I thought if it was the person who killed my father...or Chrissy, you'd want to know."

Harrison ground his teeth. "You don't have to apologize, Honey. You did the right thing."

She bit down on her bottom lip and hugged her arms around herself, then nodded. She looked shaken and exhausted.

Harrison forgot that he shouldn't touch her or get involved or that they might be on the opposite sides of this case when it was over. Or that his mother would have a fit if he knew he actually cared about Honey Granger.

And he was starting to care for her.

That thought made his gut pinch with fear, but he ignored it and pulled her against him. "Are you okay?" he asked in a gruff voice.

Honey leaned her head against his chest, her breathing erratic. "Yes," she said so softly that he barely heard her.

But the courage in that voice and in the way she'd responded to everything that had gone wrong in her life aroused his admiration again. In his mind, he saw her as that skinny, frail, lonely little girl who was cast aside by her mother and classmates.

Saw her father raising his hand to her as he imagined he'd done a dozen or more times.

Saw her running from the football field that day she'd fallen in the mud.

He'd done nothing then.

He would make up for it now.

Guilt, need and fierce protective instincts surged through him, and he lifted her chin with his thumb and searched her face.

"You aren't hurt?"

She shook her head. "There's glass everywhere inside, but I'm fine."

Except she wasn't fine and they both knew it.

"I'm going to find out who did this," Harrison said. "I won't let anyone hurt you, Honey."

She started to say something but he stopped her. "Shh." He pressed his finger to her lips to quiet her. "I mean it. People in this town haven't been nice to you and it's not right. I should have stood up for you a long time ago, when we were kids."

A blush stained her face and she averted her eyes as if bad memories had assaulted her.

"I'm sorry, I didn't mean to remind you of the past."

"I can't ever forget the past," Honey said. "Not until we figure out if my father killed your sister."

The mention of his sister twisted his insides,

but he knew now without a shadow of a doubt that Honey had suffered because of Chrissy's disappearance. That she had cared about his sister and would never have covered up for her father if she'd known that he hurt her.

Their gazes locked. Tension escalated. Emotions and desires flamed between them.

She shivered and Harrison realized he'd wanted to soothe and protect and touch her ever since he'd seen her at the morgue.

No longer able to resist, he stroked her cheek with the back of his thumb, then lowered his head and kissed her.

# Chapter Nine

Honey had wanted to kiss Harrison ever since she was sixteen.

His body felt hard and strong, his mouth hungry and eager but so gentle that tears pooled behind her eyelids.

She blinked them away and leaned into him. His hands stroked her back a second before he pulled her closer against him. She clutched his arms, suddenly dizzy, her world turning upside down as if she'd been swept up in a windstorm.

He deepened the kiss, his lips moving over hers. Her heart raced as he plunged his tongue deep inside her mouth.

Desire, need and hunger bolted through her, and she lost herself in the moment. She couldn't remember when she'd been kissed like this or when she'd even wanted to be kissed like this.

But Harrison's kiss made her feel alive. Her blood seemed hotter, her body achy, and need pulsed through her.

He lowered his hands, slid them over her hips and pulled her tighter. So tight she felt his hard length press against her belly.

But her common sense kicked in, whispering to her.

She couldn't—shouldn't—be kissing Harrison

Hawk. He was the sheriff, for God's sake. He was trying to hang her father for murder.

His mother hated her.

And she hated Tumbleweed. She'd be leaving as soon as possible. Her life was in Austin.

The wind whistled around her, clearing her head, and she pulled away from Harrison. He gripped her waist, but she took a step back.

"Stop, Harrison, we can't do this."

His breath puffed out, erratic and unsteady. "I'm sorry. That was...out of line."

"Yes, it was," she said, regretting the words when he winced as if she'd slapped him. But she didn't apologize. It was better this way.

"I'm here to cremate my father and get rid of his house," she said, reminding them both that romance—or a one-night stand—didn't fit with her plans. Or his.

"I know," he said, his voice rough with what she assumed was regret. "It won't happen again."

"No, it won't," Honey said. "I'm not the person everyone made me out to be in high school. I don't sleep around." She wiped her sweaty palms on her robe, well aware that her nipples had tightened to hard buds beneath her gown. Had he felt it?

"I didn't—"

"Let's just drop it," she said, willing herself not to reach for him again. She felt safe in his arms. Safe and wanted and void of the shame and ridicule of the town.

Harrison Hawk was strong and protective and honest and handsome—everything she'd ever wanted in a man.

Everything she couldn't have, especially considering their pasts.

"I called you because someone was outside," she said, desperately trying to steer them back on track.

He shuffled, rubbed his chin and glanced toward the window. "I looked around but no one was out there. Did you see who it was?"

Honey shook her head. "It was too dark. And I was afraid to get too close to the window for fear of getting hit."

"That was smart," Harrison said.

Or cowardly, Honey thought.

"Some of the other houses out here have been vandalized," Harrison said. "Both houses next door had windows shattered, too. So it's possible that this was just some teenagers."

Honey nodded, although in light of the fact that her father was murdered and she'd already received one threat, it seemed too coincidental.

"You really believe that?" Honey asked.

Harrison shrugged. "I said it's possible. I'll collect the rocks and send them to the lab for analysis. If it's kids, we'll probably find prints."

"Thanks, Harrison."

He nodded, then hurried to his car and returned a minute later with a crime scene kit.

Honey went inside and started a pot of coffee.

There was no way she could go back to sleep now. Not after being awakened by whoever had been out there.

And not when her body was still tingling from Harrison's kiss.

HARRISON CURSED HIMSELF for kissing Honey.

Just because he was drawn to her didn't mean she was attracted to him. For God's sake, he was supposed to be doing his job, not acting on impulses driven by his libido.

Honey had every reason to despise him and his family. They had treated her unfairly. And now here he was, getting warrants to search her property to find evidence to prove that her father was a murderer.

Even though Honey acted tough, labeling her father as a killer would hurt her.

He had to keep his distance. Besides, he did not push himself on any woman who didn't want him.

And Honey had made it clear she didn't.

Setting his jaw firmly, he phoned his deputy and asked him to pick up the search warrants for the Grangers' land, then strode up the step to the porch.

Dawn streaked the sky, the morning light illuminating the bleak condition of the house. The scent of strong coffee brewing and pine cleaner hit him as he entered. He scanned the living room area. It looked as if Honey had emptied shelves and cleaned, but shards of broken glass were scattered across the floor from the rock's impact. He took pictures of the windows, floor and glass shards.

Then he yanked on rubber gloves, opened his kit and removed evidence bags. He picked the first rock up and placed it in the bag, then put the second one in another bag.

Anger rolled through him at the sight of more glass in the laundry room and Granger's room. Glass was also scattered across the bed where Honey had been sleeping.

He knotted his hands into fists. Even if this was teenage vandals, they could have hurt Honey.

Furious, he photographed the damage.

By the time he finished, Honey was sipping coffee in the kitchen. She looked pensive as she gazed through the back window at the woods.

"My deputy should be here soon with the warrants."

Honey turned toward him, her slender face pale. But that spunky determination he'd seen in her eyes before, glimmered again, stronger than ever.

"Would you like some coffee?"

He did, but considering the tension between them, he didn't want to linger or be too friendly. "I'll pass."

She pushed a mug toward him. "Don't be silly, Harrison. I woke you up. The least I can do is give you coffee."

He accepted the mug with a muttered thanks, but didn't make eye contact. The more he looked at her, the more he wanted this mess to go away so he could kiss her again.

But she didn't want that.

So he took the mug outside with him and walked the property, searching for a clue to lead him to the person who'd terrified Honey tonight.

HONEY HAD TO distract herself from Harrison so she quickly changed into jeans and a T-shirt, then vigorously swept and cleaned up the glass. Her bed was more difficult so she stripped the bedding, rolled it up and took it outside to shake out the glass before putting it in the wash.

His deputy arrived a few minutes later, and Harrison introduced them. Mitchell Bronson was tall, dark and handsome.

But he didn't stir feelings inside her like Harrison did.

He shook her hand, his friendly smile putting her at ease. "Sorry about your trouble, ma'am. The sheriff and I will do everything we can to find out who did this."

"Thank you."

"We're going to search the property now," Harrison said.

Honey's heart thumped.

Harrison descended the step from the porch, followed by the deputy. She watched them comb the area in front of the house, then they moved to the left side.

Honey shoveled up more glass from the back hallway, praying he didn't find Chrissy.

For the past few years, she'd tried to forget everything about this town and this house and her father, but now she struggled to recall details about Chrissy.

How many times had she stopped by? One. Two. Maybe three?

The night she disappeared, Chrissy had sneaked out with her brother Brayden and followed Harrison to the bluff. Someone there said Chrissy left and came to Honey's.

But Honey didn't see Chrissy that night at her house because she'd also sneaked out to the bluff and hidden like a voyeur at the edge of the woods, watching the party. Watching Harrison.

Although she'd never told anyone that.

She'd felt lonely and too scared to join in because she'd known she didn't belong.

Just as she didn't belong now.

What if Chrissy had come to her house while she was gone and her father had been so drunk he'd taken his anger out on Chrissy?

If she'd stayed home that night, she could have protected Chrissy.

HARRISON AND HIS deputy searched every corner of the woods, looked near tree stumps, checked uneven patches of ground in case Granger had buried her, and examined the yard and crawl space.

"She's not here," Deputy Bronson said.

Harrison heaved a sigh of relief. As much as he wanted to find Chrissy, he'd harbored hope that somehow she'd survived. Although that thought was terrifying in itself. Kidnap victims who were found after years of captivity often suffered from trauma, amnesia or Stockholm syndrome.

"Sheriff, you okay?"

His deputy's voice jarred him from his thoughts. "Yeah."

His phone buzzed, and he checked the number. The lab. "Let me get this, then we'll tell Honey that we're leaving."

"Honey?"

"Miss Granger," he said, realizing the way he'd said her name sounded personal. Harrison punched Connect and Bronson headed to his car while he walked toward the house. "Sheriff Hawk."

"It's Regan Willis from the lab. I have results on that ribbon you dropped off."

"Yeah?"

"The hair caught in the ribbon definitely matched your sister's, Harrison."

He sucked in a breath, grateful that the former sheriff had kept Chrissy's hairbrush so they could compare it for a match.

"There's more. I found traces of a chemical that is only found in the caves at the bluff."

"I know she was there," he said.

Which meant Granger had either been at the

caves that night and possibly killed Chrissy there, or she'd come to the Grangers' house and he'd killed her, then took her to another spot to bury her.

Or she could have come to the Grangers' house, lost the ribbon outside, then a stranger had picked her up and Granger later found the ribbon.

Dammit, he was grasping.

"What about the button?" Harrison asked.

"Some DNA but it doesn't match anyone in the system." She paused. "But I can tell you that it belonged to a female."

Hell, it could have been another teenage girl up at the bluff. Or…his mother…

No, his mother wouldn't have gone to the bluff. Unless she went looking for Chrissy after she'd learned Chrissy was missing.

He explained about the attack on Honey's house. "I'll drop the rocks off for you to analyze. But I'm heading to the bluff first to check those caves."

"Good luck, Sheriff. Let me know if I can do anything else."

He thanked her and hung up. By the time he reached Honey's house, she was coming outside.

"Did you find anything?" she asked.

He shook his head. "I'm going to the bluff to search the caves." He gestured toward the windows. "I'll come back later and board up the windows for you."

"I can take care of that myself," Honey said. "I

need to go into town to meet the director of the crematorium anyway, so I'll pick up supplies."

He remembered the look of fear in her eyes when he'd first arrived. "I don't think whoever did this will come back during the day. But let me know if you need me."

Honey's withering look indicated that was the last thing she intended to do.

Resigned, he strode to his SUV and drove to the bluff. The sooner he found answers, the sooner Honey could leave and return to Austin.

Did she have someone special waiting for her there?

He grunted and parked at the bluff, then climbed out to meet his deputy. It didn't matter if she did.

Nothing could happen between them.

"Where do we start?" Deputy Bronson asked.

Harrison noted a few kids hanging out at the swimming hole. Although it was only midday, the heat had already climbed, the sun blazing. Technically this area was a crime scene. He should shut it down to the students and others who liked to hike the trails into the mountain.

But they'd need serious manpower to keep people away.

If Chrissy was killed here, they'd also have to weed through eighteen years of locals and strangers on the grounds and in the caves. A near-impossible task.

In spite of the sunlight, the caves were dark inside, so he grabbed his flashlight. Bronson did the same and they started at the mouth of the cave.

"What are we looking for?" Bronson asked.

Harrison explained about the ribbon, and that he'd found the rock/murder weapon used on Granger. "We never found my sister's backpack or jacket or anything of hers," he said. "So keep an eye out for any clothing or items that may have belonged to a child."

"You know the teens like to camp out here," Bronson said. "And there are a couple of homeless men who use it for shelter in the winter."

"I know," Harrison said. "I found the rock used to kill Granger. Not sure if the other stuff belonged to the killer or if the killer just hid the murder weapon here." Harrison gestured to the section of burned wood, a water canteen, discarded blanket and cigarette stubs. "Bag all that stuff and send it to the lab."

Together they sorted through the stuff and bagged it, then Bronson took it to his car and locked it inside.

Back inside the tunnel, they parted, veering in different directions. The caves had once been mined and consisted of a maze of underground tunnels that spanned about three miles.

The air felt hot and stale, the scent of urine and a dead animal permeating the space. He shone his light along the walls, searching the corners and dirt. Cigarette stubs, discarded water bottles and a few liquor bottles and beer cans had been left throughout. He filled a trash bag with the items, then veered into the last area, a room at the end of the tunnel, which had once been mined.

He raked his flashlight across the wooden stakes marking areas where the workers had dug. Something shimmered beneath the beam of his flashlight. A streak of yellow.

His breath froze in his lungs.

Yellow. Another ribbon.

Fear seized him, and he stalked forward, knelt and zeroed in on the tip of the yellow.

It was a ribbon. Just like Chrissy's.

Only part of it was buried in the dirt.

Emotions flooded him and for a moment, he couldn't breathe. Couldn't move.

Had someone killed Chrissy and buried her here in this cave?

# Chapter Ten

Harrison raked dirt away from where the strip of yellow poked through.

His lungs squeezed for air. After all this time, was he going to find Chrissy's body beneath the dirt and rocks?

It looked as if there had been a rockslide inside the cave in this area, so he moved several stones aside and tugged the ribbon free.

It definitely matched the one he'd found at Honey's.

Sweat beaded his neck, and he studied the rock pile. He had to dig deeper.

Nerves raw, he strode back through the cave, this time shining his light to see if there were any more sections on the ground that looked uneven, as if they might be burial spots, but he didn't find anything.

When he reached the mouth of the cave, he breathed in the fresh air, then rushed to his SUV and retrieved a shovel from the back. Gripping it with clammy hands, he hurried back inside the cave to the far end where he'd found the ribbon. He checked the area to make sure the walls wouldn't collapse when he dug, and decided it was safe. Wall supports had been built when the miners had worked the cave.

Then he began to dig.

Rocks, pebbles and dirt formed a small mound. Jaw set, he lifted one shovel full of debris, then another until he reached the ground beneath. He ran his hand over it and felt a small bump. God help him, he wanted answers.

But he didn't want to find his sister's body.

Resigned, he jammed the shovel into the ground and dug, moving dirt to create a hole. He continued digging two feet, then three, but the space was empty.

Relief flooded him. Chrissy wasn't here.

He stood, wiping dirt and sweat from his face with the back of his sleeve, then headed back outside.

His deputy was waiting at the mouth of the cave.

"Did you find anything?" Harrison asked.

"Afraid not," Bronson said. "You?"

Harrison removed the ribbon from his pocket. "This belonged to my sister."

"So she was here?"

Harrison rarely talked about that night, but he assumed Bronson had heard some version of it.

"We knew she came to the bluff," Harrison said. "Brayden and she sneaked out. They were exploring the caves when Brayden tripped and hurt his ankle. Chrissy was supposed to go get help, but was never seen again."

"I'm sorry, man," Bronson said. "That must have been rough."

Harrison gave a clipped nod, but his cell phone buzzed with a text, saving him from having to respond.

It was from Lucas.

Geoffrey Williams meeting us at your office. Half an hour.

Harrison sent a return text saying he'd be there. "Bronson, ride by the Grangers' place and make sure there's no more trouble there."

Bronson agreed, and Harrison hurried to his SUV. If Lucas had suspicions about Geoffrey Williams, Harrison had to interrogate the man.

Although he wasn't looking forward to it. Geoffrey Williams was well liked and served on the town council.

He wouldn't like any questions that remotely suggested he'd done something illegal.

HONEY HAD EXPERIENCE yielding a hammer. She found some plywood in the garage and boarded up the windows.

Stepping back to look at it, she realized that covering the windows meant the house was pitched in darkness inside.

A shiver rippled up her spine.

Boarding the window meant no one could look

inside, but it also prevented her from looking out and made her feel claustrophobic.

The only way to solve the problem was to completely replace the windows, but to do that, she needed to repair rotting wood and casings, which meant committing to more improvements.

Even if she renovated her father's house, it would be a hard sell. One look at the surrounding yards and dilapidated houses in the neighborhood would scare away potential buyers.

She finished with the windows, then went to stow the hammer in the garage when she noticed a box of old junk. Yard tools and plant pots had been tossed into the box along with old work gloves and a broken picture frame.

Harrison had searched the garage, but when she moved the box to haul it toward the door to carry it to the junkyard, she spotted a small wooden box wedged in the back. She slid it from the shelf and set it on the workbench, then opened it.

An assortment of loose change filled the box.

Relief flooded her when she realized there was nothing of Chrissy's inside. But she scrounged through the coins and found an old photograph in the bottom of the box.

Her chest squeezed.

She'd forgotten what her mother looked like, but now she realized she looked a lot like her. Her mother had the same honey-blond hair and brown eyes, although she looked sickly thin and dark circles shadowed her eyes.

Pain rippled through her—her mother had left when she was seven.

Had her father turned his anger on her because she reminded him of his wife?

She traced a finger over her mother's face, aching for what she'd wanted and never had.

Why hadn't her mother taken her with her when she'd left?

Was she that unlovable?

HARRISON MET LUCAS at the sheriff's office. Geoffrey Williams was waiting with him, his impeccable suit and designer shoes a sign he had money and wanted others to know it.

So opposite of Harrison and his brothers, who were focused on family and justice.

Williams buttoned his jacket as he stood, then extended his hand. "What can I do for you, Sheriff?"

Harrison shook his hand. "Lucas didn't tell you what this was about?"

Lucas kept a straight face. "I just explained that he might be able to help us with something."

Williams arched a brow. "I am your town councilman. Always happy to be of service."

The damn man was acting as if he hadn't attended school with Harrison and Lucas, as if his blue blood made him a class above the Hawks.

"Good, then have a seat," Harrison said. "We want to talk to you about the night my sister went missing."

Shock flashed in Williams's eyes. "What? Why? That was years ago."

"Yes, but her case has never been solved," Harrison said.

"I'm sorry about that," Williams said, "but I'm not sure how I can help." Williams's eyes narrowed. He was a thin man, his face long, his chin strong, his hands manicured.

"In fact, didn't I hear that Mr. Granger died?" Williams continued. "I thought your family believed he had something to do with your sister's disappearance."

"That was one theory," Harrison said.

Lucas folded his arms, adopting his federal agent demeanor. "Harrison and I have been reviewing everything that happened, Geoffrey. You were at the bluff that night."

A wary look snapped in Williams's gray eyes. "Yes, along with a dozen other teenagers. Are you talking to all of them?"

"Yes," Harrison said bluntly.

Williams squared his shoulders in a defensive gesture. "You know Sheriff Dunar questioned all of us. Why don't you read his report?"

"I have," Harrison said.

"So have I," Lucas added in a solemn voice. "But one thing is bothering me."

Williams's eyes darted back and forth between them as if he suspected they were trying to trap him. "What's that?"

Lucas cleared his throat. "You told the sheriff that you saw Chrissy but that you didn't speak to her."

Williams crossed his leg, chin lifted. "Yes. I was meeting Tina Fuller, not paying attention to your kid sister."

Harrison's jaw tightened. "What was she doing when you saw her?"

"Lurking around behind some rocks," Williams said. "Spying on us like she was a tattletale going to get us in trouble." He quickly realized how his comment sounded and added, "Not that we were doing anything wrong. Having a few beers, but it was the first day of summer break."

Memories of that long, hot summer bombarded Harrison. Days on end of searching the woods and posting fliers and…arguments between his parents.

"You're lying." Lucas's stone-cold expression was a sign of the tough interrogator and agent Harrison had suspected his brother was, although he'd yet to see him in action.

Anger replaced the coolness in Williams's eyes. "How dare you suggest that, Lucas. We were friends."

That was the problem. Harrison and Lucas both knew Williams. And didn't trust him.

"I've done everything I can to help this community," Williams continued, "and I've tried to bring revenue back to this fledgling hole in the wall—"

"You're forgetting that I knew you back then, Geoffrey," Lucas said. "You were always showing off, trying to impress everyone, especially the girls. You did meet up with Tina, then you saw my sister sneaking around and you went over and started making fun of her. You called her names, then you shoved her and told her to leave you alone."

The color faded from Williams's face. "We were just kids," he said. "If I pushed her, it was innocent. For God's sake, I didn't hurt her."

"Maybe, maybe not." Lucas leaned over, jamming his face into Williams's in an intimidating gesture. "Maybe she didn't listen and you and Tina sneaked off to make out and Chrissy followed. She was my sister and I loved her, but she could be annoying. Maybe she interrupted you and Tina, and you pushed her again, except this time she fell and hurt her head."

"It could have been an accident," Harrison cut in, following Lucas's lead. "She fell and was hurt or maybe worse, and you panicked." Although that wouldn't explain how Chrissy's ribbon ended up at Honey's. Unless she'd lost it that night, and Granger had found it and taken it home.

Still, something didn't fit.

Williams stood, rolled his shoulders then gave them both a cool look. "Listen to me. I did not kill your sister. Now, if you want to talk to me again, call my lawyer." He shoved a business card at Harrison.

Harrison met the man's gaze with a challenge,

and Williams dropped the card on the desk, then strode out, carrying an air of authority with him.

"Damn," Lucas said.

"You think he's telling the truth?" Harrison asked.

"Hell if I know." Lucas stripped his tie and rubbed his neck. "But I'm going to talk with Tina Fuller. If Williams did something to Chrissy and Tina knows, maybe the guilt over keeping quiet is catching up with her."

QUESTIONS ABOUT HER mother needled Honey.

Had her father tried to convince her not to leave? Where had she gone? Had he tried to find her?

*She* hadn't.

She'd figured if her mother wanted to be with her, she wouldn't have abandoned her.

Unless her mother had been afraid of Honey's father—if so, why leave her child with the man?

The one person who might know was the former sheriff. He'd been called out to their house on numerous occasions.

She wanted to leave Tumbleweed but she couldn't do that without answers. And the only way to get them was to ask questions of her own.

She parked at Harrison's office, shoulders tense as she walked up to the door and went in. Harrison was standing at his desk as if ready to leave, another man beside him.

Lucas.

All of the Hawk men were handsome, although Harrison was always the most striking to her, but Lucas was good-looking. As a teen his smile and dimples had persuaded teachers to let him off the hook when he was in trouble.

Old insecurities nearly sent her running back to her van. But the logo on the outside reminded her that she was successful now. She didn't have to prove herself to anyone.

"Honey, what are you doing here?" Harrison asked.

"That's what I want to know."

Honey froze at the harsh sound of Mrs. Hawk's voice behind her. She braced herself by silently counting to ten.

"Mom." Harrison held up a warning hand. "Let me handle this."

Lucas's curious gaze fell on her. "Hello, Honey. I'm sorry about your father."

She breathed a little easier. Lucas hadn't lost his charm.

"Now that your father is dead, did you decide to tell the truth about what he did to our little Chrissy?" Mrs. Hawk asked.

Fury and hurt engulfed Honey. Mrs. Hawk hadn't lost her hatred for her. God help her, she was sick and tired of people in Tumbleweed judging her.

The gossip she'd heard at the diner echoed in her head.

She whirled around. "I told the truth—I didn't

see Chrissy that night and I certainly never saw my father hurt her."

Mrs. Hawk took a step closer, her anger palpable. "You always were a little liar. You and your father tore our family apart. My husband left because of Chrissy—"

"Speaking of lying," Honey said, cutting her off. "Why don't you tell the truth about the real reason your husband left you?"

The woman paled. Harrison's boots pounded the floor as he crossed the room; Lucas followed.

Honey's gaze met Mrs. Hawk's. She had been vehement toward Honey, but now she'd clammed up.

"I don't know what you're talking about," Mrs. Hawk said in a brittle tone.

Honey arched a brow. "Really? Because I heard that the night Chrissy went missing, you and your husband had a fight at that party. A fight—"

Mrs. Hawk raised her hand and slapped Honey. The sharp sting made her jerk her head back.

Harrison grabbed his mother's arm and pulled her away. "Mother, what the hell?"

"Let's calm down," Lucas said in a low voice.

"Get out of here, Honey. You don't belong in Tumbleweed," Mrs. Hawk snarled.

"Don't worry. I hate this town as much as you hate me," Honey said. "But I'm not a liar. Tell your sons about the fight."

"What is she talking about?" Harrison asked.

"Nothing." Mrs. Hawk rubbed Harrison's arm.

He looked up at Honey with troubled eyes. "Honey?"

"You were always judging me," she said to his mother, her chest heaving. "So tell them about your affair."

Shock bolted across Harrison's and Lucas's faces.

"Mother?" Harrison and Lucas asked at the same time.

Mrs. Hawk squeezed her eyes shut for a moment as if struggling to decide how to respond.

Honey hated causing Harrison pain, but there was no turning back now. If they were going to get answers, they had to explore every angle. And they might have to face hard truths.

If Mrs. Hawk's affair had something to do with Chrissy's paternity, it might also have something to do with her disappearance.

## Chapter Eleven

Harrison felt as if he'd been hit by a two-by-four.

"What are you talking about, Honey?"

Emotions darkened her eyes. "I'm sorry, Harrison. I shouldn't have said anything."

Except she *had* said something.

He turned to his mother, who looked shell-shocked. "Mother?"

Lucas cleared his throat and took his mother's arm. "Mom, what's going on?"

"I don't have to answer to *her*," his mother said vehemently.

An uneasy feeling clawed at Harrison's stomach. "But you do have to answer to us. We're your sons."

"I know that," his mother said. "But what happened between me and your father was our business."

"Not if it had something to do with the night Chrissy disappeared," Harrison said.

Lucas crossed his arms, his voice low, controlled. But filled with turmoil. "Or the reason he left us."

Harrison couldn't agree more. "That's right. What happened, Mother?"

She gestured toward Honey. "I don't intend to discuss my marriage or private life with her in the room."

Pain streaked Honey's eyes. "Fine. I'll leave. But I need to talk to you when you're finished, Harrison."

"Did you find something else at the house?" Harrison asked, then realized that he hadn't told his mother about the ribbon.

"No. But I still need to talk to you." She crossed the room and reached for the doorknob. "I'll wait outside."

He gave a quick nod, then glanced back at his mother. She was looking at the door as if she wanted to run.

"Mother," Lucas said. "Tell us the truth. What happened at that party?"

His mother fisted her hands by her sides. Her brows were pinched, her mouth tight. "Your father and I did argue. Married couples fight sometimes."

Harrison leaned against his desk, his gaze scrutinizing her. "You fought about the fact that you had an affair?"

A tense second stretched into an awkward moment, which Harrison took as a yes.

"Who was it with?" Lucas asked, his thoughts obviously on track with Harrison's.

"It doesn't matter. It happened a long time ago. It meant nothing."

"But Dad was upset about it," Harrison said. "When was the affair? Around the time Chrissy disappeared?"

She shoved a strand of hair behind her ear, her hand trembling. "No, it was long before that. Years before."

"YEARS BEFORE?" HARRISON SAID, suspicion sneaking up on him. "How many years?"

Their mother fiddled with her purse strap, avoiding eye contact. "Eleven," she said so quietly that for a moment Harrison thought he'd imagined it.

"Eleven?" Lucas said in a low voice. "And Chrissy was ten…"

The truth dawned on Harrison in a sickening rush. "Chrissy… She wasn't Dad's child?"

A low sob rumbled from his mother's throat, and tears blurred her eyes as she looked at them. "No… I'm sorry… I never wanted you boys to find out."

"Is that why he left us?" Lucas pressed. "Because he discovered Chrissy wasn't his daughter?"

A wary resignation settled on their mother's face. "No, he left because he wanted to find Chrissy."

Harrison's investigative mind kicked in, the ramifications quickly adding up. "Did he suspect that Chrissy's biological father took her?"

"He wanted to talk to him," she said. "But I assured him that he wouldn't do such a thing. He wanted Steven to raise Chrissy as his own."

"Why would he want that?" Lucas asked.

"It's complicated," his mother whispered.

"What about Chrissy?" Harrison cut in. "Did she know?"

"No…at least I don't think so."

Harrison struggled to keep his temper in check. "What if she heard you and Dad talking and realized she had another father? Perhaps she decided to find him?"

"Maybe that's the reason she didn't come home," Lucas suggested. "She went to confront him."

"And things didn't go well," Harrison said. Anger railed inside him. All this time he'd blamed himself for his father leaving. For losing Chrissy to a possible predator.

"Did Dad talk to this man?" Harrison asked.

"No," his mother said. "He left in a rage and… he just never came back."

"You didn't hear from him again?" Lucas said. "No phone calls or a note?"

"Nothing," she cried. "I knew he was upset about the indiscretion, but it happened so long ago that I thought we'd already gotten past it. He loved Chrissy like she was his own daughter and she adored him."

"Who was the man?" Lucas asked.

"I don't intend to tell you," their mother said. "Like I said, it was over a long time ago."

"But what if he had something to do with Chrissy's disappearance? Perhaps she went to see him and he was afraid she'd tell everyone and ruin his life or marriage—"

"It wasn't like that at all." She raised a warning finger to him then to Lucas. "I'm telling you—you boys need to drop it."

"Why should we?" Harrison asked. "You're quick to point the finger at Honey and her father when you're the one who's been keeping secrets all these years. A secret that might have led us to the truth about Chrissy."

His mother met Harrison's gaze with the stern look that had made him stop in his tracks as a kid. He'd never wanted to disappoint her or his father. And when he had, he'd mentally beaten himself up.

"I blamed myself because he left," Harrison admitted in a gruff voice.

Lucas grimaced. "And I blamed myself, Mom."

Regret wrenched her face. "I'm sorry, boys. I never meant for you to do that. But…you have to let this be."

"We need answers about Chrissy," Harrison said.

"So do I." She feathered her bangs away from her forehead with trembling fingers. "But Chrissy's biological father had nothing to do with her disappearance. Trust me, he's a good man and wanted her to be happy in our family."

"Did you ask him?" Lucas said.

She nodded. "Of course. He was upset that she was missing. But he hadn't seen or spoken with her."

With one last sharp look, she strode out the door.

Harrison's pulse pounded. Trust her?

How could they do that when she'd lied to them their whole lives?

HONEY CLENCHED HER hands together as she sat on the park bench outside the sheriff's office.

She shouldn't have confronted Harrison's mother. The hurt on Harrison's face…

The door swung open, and Mrs. Hawk appeared, clutching her purse as if it was a weapon. She stared at Honey, her condescending expression tearing at Honey.

"I'm sorry, Mrs. Hawk," she said softly. "I shouldn't have said anything. I was angry and upset, but it doesn't excuse it."

The woman's eyes narrowed suspiciously as if she sensed Honey had some ulterior motive.

"I didn't mean to hurt your sons or you," Honey continued, determined not to let the woman turn her into a bitter person. She wanted to be strong, but not vindictive or mean or hurtful.

Lord knows she'd been on the receiving end of gossip and she understood how it could eat at a person's heart and soul.

"What do you want?" Mrs. Hawk asked.

Honey released a shaky breath. "Just the truth, like you do."

"No, I want my daughter back. Even the truth won't do that."

The anguish in the woman's voice wrenched Honey's heart. Losing her father was hard, but they hadn't been close. She couldn't imagine losing a child.

"I'm sorry," Honey said. "I can't imagine how painful it is to lose a daughter."

"No, you can't." Mrs. Hawk wiped at a tear seeping from her eye, then her frown returned.

"I won't let you take my son or sons from me," she said, the vehemence back. "So don't even try."

Honey opened her mouth to reassure her that she wasn't out to take one of her sons, but Harrison stepped outside and she bit back a response as the woman hurried to her vehicle.

Tires squealed as she sped down the street.

A muscle ticked in Harrison's jaw. Regret for hurting him made tears prick at her eyes. Harrison was a good man, a man full of passion and honor.

"I'm sorry," she said, standing to face him. "I shouldn't have confronted your mother. I…didn't mean to upset you, Harrison."

His stormy gaze met hers. The closeness she'd felt with him the night before was gone. The kiss seemed a million years ago.

"I'm going to talk to Sheriff Dunar," he said, ignoring her and her apology.

"I want to talk to him, too," Honey said.

His brows furrowed. "You need to stay out of this."

"I can't," Honey said. "Everyone in Tumbleweed thinks my father is a murderer. Even I'm questioning him and wondering about my mother's disappearance."

"What do you mean?"

Honey shrugged. "I thought she ran off, but if he was more violent than I realized, what if he did something to her?"

Harrison's head was still spinning from the revelations about his mother's affair. He and Lucas planned to meet Dexter and Brayden for a beer later and fill them in.

He dreaded that conversation, but they had a right to know.

Dexter might be able to use his detective skills to find out the identity of their mother's lover. And they would find out, even if they had to follow her.

Most likely she would contact the man and give him a heads-up.

"Harrison?"

He jerked back to reality. Honey was talking. She'd apologized. She wanted to talk to the sheriff about her father and mother.

Under the circumstances, her questions seemed valid.

He admired the fact that she wanted the truth enough to face it, even if it was ugly.

"Let's go." He strode toward his SUV, not bothering to wait on Honey. She followed him silently, the mood tense as he drove toward the lake where the former sheriff had retired.

He clenched the steering wheel in a white-knuckle grip. He couldn't talk about the situation with Honey or his mother right now, not when his mother's reaction was too fresh in his mind.

She was definitely protecting the man she'd had an affair with. Why?

Because she still cared for him?

She said she'd talked to him after Chrissy went missing and he wasn't responsible. But she must have suspected that he had something to do with her disappearance or she wouldn't have asked him.

HONEY RUBBED HER cheek as they drove, her face still stinging from the slap she'd received.

"Are you okay?" Harrison asked in a gruff voice.

She twisted her head to look at him and dropped her hand to her lap. "Yes. I've had worse."

He winced. "I'm sorry. My mother had no right to hit you. I... I've never seen her like that."

"She didn't spank you when you were young?"

Harrison shook his head. "No, my father was the one with the temper."

"I seem to bring out the worst in her," Honey said in a low voice.

Harrison worked his mouth from side to side. "I know. I don't understand it."

She did—his mother thought she was protecting her sons from Honey, the bad girl.

But she knew nothing about Honey or the woman she'd become.

Harrison veered down a narrow dirt road that wove through the woods.

"Sheriff Dunar lives out here?"

He nodded. "When he retired, he and his wife wanted to live by the lake."

"It's pretty," Honey said. "I'd forgotten how close Tumbleweed is to the lake."

And to her father's house. If she decided to redo it and sell, the lake could be a marketing point.

The SUV rumbled over the rough terrain, and she noted a few rustic houses built along the way. If people wanted privacy and a retreat in the woods by the lake, this was the place.

They broke to a clearing where a small cabin sat, a black pickup parked in front. A gray-haired woman was tending a garden to the right.

Harrison parked and climbed out, and Honey followed.

"Mrs. Dunar," Harrison said. "Is your husband here?"

The woman shaded her eyes with one hand, a garden trowel in her other. "Sure is. Fishing on the dock out back."

"Thanks."

Honey followed Harrison around the side of the cabin. The sheriff had aged since she'd left town. His face was thin, but his belly had grown rounder. He pushed his hat back and peered at them.

"Well, well, Sheriff Hawk, I heard you found Waylon Granger dead. I figured you'd show up here sometime." He glanced at Honey with narrowed eyes, then a frown marred his face. "You're his kid, aren't you?"

Honey nodded. "Yes, I came back to handle funeral arrangements."

He set his fishing pole aside. "I'm sorry for your loss."

Honey murmured thanks, the moment awkward.

"So what can I help you with?" Sheriff Dunar asked.

"I have questions about when my mother left," Honey said.

"And I want to talk about my sister's disappearance." Harrison explained that Honey's father was murdered.

The older man pulled at his chin. "You got any theories about who killed Granger?" he asked Harrison.

"I think his murder may have something to do with Chrissy," Harrison said. "Honey found one of my sister's hair ribbons in her father's house."

"So you think Granger killed Chrissy?"

"It's one theory. We searched his property but didn't find anything. Although I found her other hair ribbon in the mine."

The sheriff frowned. "We searched those mines and all around the bluff," he said, "and didn't find anything."

"The ribbon was half-buried in rubble inside the cave," Harrison said. "You questioned all the teenagers at the bluff that night, didn't you?"

"Yes, I made notes in my police report."

"Did anyone stand out to you or seem suspicious?" Harrison asked.

The sheriff folded his hands and laid them on his belly. "Well, there was one guy, a homeless drifter, who used to sleep in the park and at the bluff. I thought he might have seen something, but two weeks after I talked to him, he turned up dead."

The timing was interesting. "What was COD?"

"Liver failure," the sheriff said. "Poor guy died in his sleep."

"What about the teenagers?" Harrison asked.

"All the kids seemed nervous, but I assumed that was just because your sister disappeared. Something like that shakes up the whole town." He paused and worked the inside of his cheek with his tongue. "Honestly, I thought the incident might spook some of the teenagers enough to stay away from the bluff. I always thought that swimming hole and the ridge were dangerous."

Honey made a low sound in her throat. "Mrs. Hawk thought Chrissy came to my house. Did you question my father?"

He nodded, his thick brows meeting in the middle of his forehead. "Yeah, we talked."

"And?" Honey held her breath.

The sheriff sighed. "He was drunk as a skunk the next morning when I stopped by to talk to him. Said he didn't go anywhere the night before."

If only she'd stayed home, she'd know for sure if he'd left. Or if Chrissy had come by to see her.

The memory of that morning still disturbed Honey. She'd been terrified her father would catch her sneaking back in the house in the middle of the night, but he was passed out and hadn't stirred.

"Did he act suspicious when you talked to him?" Harrison asked.

"That's hard to say," Sheriff Dunar said. "When he was drunk, he got belligerent. But I didn't see signs of foul play at the house."

Honey swallowed hard. She had to summon the courage to ask him the question eating at her. "My mother left abruptly." She inhaled sharply. "Did you ever suspect that my father did something to her?"

# Chapter Twelve

Honey held her breath while she waited on the sheriff's response.

"Your daddy was a mean drunk," the sheriff said. "When your mama left, I wondered if he'd hurt her, but Waylon showed me the note she left."

"She left a note?"

He picked up a twig and snapped it in two. "Yeah. She said she couldn't take it anymore, that she'd met someone else and was leaving town."

Her father could have forged the note. "Did you keep the note?"

"Naw, but I compared the handwriting against your mama's and it was hers. And I checked the bus station, and they verified that she boarded a bus headed toward San Antonio."

Honey wasn't sure if she was relieved or disappointed. She didn't want to believe that her father had killed her mother, but it hurt to know that her mother had abandoned her and never come back.

HARRISON GLANCED ACROSS the lake, giving Honey time to absorb the sheriff's words. Honey's mother had left without telling her goodbye. He understood—his father had done the same thing.

Agitation lined her face. "I'm going to take a walk."

"Honey?" Harrison glanced at her to see if she was okay.

"I'll be back." She avoided his gaze and walked from the dock to the path leading around the lake. The summer breeze blew gently, ruffling leaves, and water rippled beneath the sun.

She looked so lost and alone that he wanted to join her and comfort her.

But he was here for information and he had to get it.

"Sheriff," he said in a low voice. "I recently learned that Chrissy was not my father's birth child. My parents argued about it the night she disappeared. Did you know anything about that argument?"

The sheriff fiddled with the button on his overalls. "No. I sensed tension between your folks and thought they might be holding something back, but they didn't mention a fight or anything about Chrissy's paternity."

Then it was up to him and his brothers to find out the man's name and talk to him.

"My brother mentioned that Geoffrey Williams was one of the teens at the bluff that night," Harrison said. "When you questioned him, did he act strange or did any of the other teens mention seeing him with Chrissy?"

The sheriff pinched the bridge of his nose. "It

was a long time ago, Harrison. Williams is on the town council. Most folks like him."

"But you don't?"

The sheriff shrugged. "He's always been too cocky for me. Back then he was a smart-ass. But if he said anything suspicious, I would have written it in my notes."

Harrison had reviewed them a dozen times, although he didn't recall anything specific about Geoffrey.

The sheriff snapped his fingers. "Although there was one thing that struck me odd. Happened a couple of years later."

"What was that?" Harrison asked.

"Another little girl went missing from Waco. She was about the same age as Chrissy."

Harrison's pulse jumped. "You think the two cases were related?"

The sheriff shrugged. "I called and talked to the detective working the case, and we didn't find any connection. But I always wondered…"

"Did they find that little girl?" Harrison asked.

The sheriff shook his head. "Afraid not."

"Were there any suspects?" Harrison asked.

"He looked at the immediate family, but they checked out."

Of course. Parents and families were always primary suspects.

"So you looked at my parents when Chrissy went missing?"

"I had to," he said. "Why, Harrison? Do you think one of them had something to do with her disappearance?"

Did he?

It had never occurred to him that that was a possibility. But knowing about the argument and his mother's affair shed a different light on the situation.

So did the fact that another little girl had disappeared from Waco.

HONEY LOST HERSELF in the beauty of the lake. She had to distract herself from her current situation.

Decisions had to be made about her father's house, but first she had to settle what to do with his remains.

She certainly didn't plan to take her father's ashes home with her to Austin.

Maybe she'd scatter them here in the lake.

Birds chirped from a tree overlooking the lake drawing her gaze to the water. The natural landscape and rustic cabins gave the property a serene, majestic look. There were also acres and acres of land that could hold lovely homes—or a retreat center—for travelers and guests visiting the area. A trail around the lake for horseback riding would be inviting and the wooded areas would offer great camping and picnic sites.

An investor could make a fortune if he developed the property right. But someone else could ruin it if he or she chose to build condos or apartments.

The wooden dock creaked as she stepped back onto it. Not that she cared what happened here. This lake was part of Tumbleweed, a place she despised.

Harrison stood as she approached, his posture rigid. He looked troubled, as if disturbed by something the sheriff had said.

She'd wanted to hear their conversation but had to take a break. She'd also sensed Harrison wanted privacy to discuss his mother's affair.

Odd that the woman had judged her so harshly when she wasn't perfect herself.

"Are you ready to go?" Harrison asked.

She was ready to leave town, but she refrained from commenting and simply nodded.

"Thank you, Sheriff. If you think of anything else, call me."

The sheriff murmured he would, and Honey followed Harrison to his SUV. "Did you learn anything?" she asked as they drove away.

"Just that a little girl went missing in Waco a short time after Chrissy did. The sheriff doesn't think she was ever found."

Honey's mind spun. "You think that the same person who took Chrissy took that girl?"

"I don't know, but it's worth looking into."

Honey twisted her hands in her lap. If that was

true, it might clear her father. He'd been drinking so much back then that he never left Tumbleweed.

HARRISON DROPPED HONEY back at her car at the sheriff's office, then drove to The Broken Spoke, the local bar, to meet his brothers.

Lucas looked antsy as he approached. Dexter and Brayden were talking to the waitress as she set a pitcher of beer and a plate of wings and basket of fries on the table.

His stomach growled, reminding him that he hadn't eaten today, and he claimed a wooden chair at the table with his brothers.

Dexter poured them each a mug of beer, then pushed one toward Harrison. "So what's this family meeting about?"

He raised a brow at Lucas, who shook his head, indicating he hadn't explained.

"A couple of things," Harrison said. "But first, Lucas, tell them about Williams."

Lucas nodded. "He denied any wrongdoing and lawyered up. I talked to Tina Fuller. She said Chrissy followed her and Geoffrey to the creek but Geoffrey shoved her and told her to leave them alone, and she ran off."

"Which way did she go?" Brayden asked.

"Toward Honey's."

Damn, they were back to Granger.

Lucas gestured to Harrison. "You want to fill them in on the rest?"

He didn't, but he had to, so he explained about their mother's affair.

"You're kidding?" The color drained from Brayden's face.

"Mom cheated on Dad?" Dexter asked, his voice cracking.

"It gets worse," Lucas said.

Brayden and Dexter looked at Harrison as if begging him to say, "It's not so," but he refused to lie to them. "Chrissy was not Dad's biological child."

Shock bolted across his brothers' faces. He and Lucas sipped their beers while they gave Dexter and Brayden time to absorb the news.

"Dad knew this?" Dexter asked.

Harrison nodded. "Mom and Dad fought about it the night Chrissy disappeared."

Brayden swallowed hard. "Did Chrissy know?"

Harrison shrugged. "Mom said they didn't tell her, but it's possible that she overheard something at some point."

"Then she could have tried to find her birth father." Dexter gripped the table edge. "Who is the bastard?"

Harrison scraped a hand through his hair. "Mom wouldn't tell us."

"This is not exactly ethical," Lucas said, "but I could put a trace on Mom's phone to see if she calls him."

"I'll talk to her," Brayden said. "Maybe I can convince her to talk."

"She seemed pretty protective of the man's identity," Lucas said.

Harrison reached for a french fry. "She also said it had been over for a very long time and insisted the man wouldn't have hurt Chrissy."

"How can we believe her when she lied all these years?" A sense of betrayal laced Dexter's voice.

"I feel the same way," Harrison said. "So what do we do?"

"I'll watch her, maybe follow her," Brayden said. "She might try to see him."

A tense silence stretched between them, filled with guilt and indecision and the reality that none of them would be happy until they knew the man's name and confirmed that he wasn't involved in their sister's disappearance.

Finally they all agreed, then dug into the wings. But Harrison couldn't get the sheriff's words out of his head. "There's something else. It might be important."

Dexter released a weary sigh. "What else?"

Harrison snatched another wing, then relayed his conversation with the sheriff.

"Another girl went missing just like our sister," Lucas said. "Why didn't he mention this before?"

"He didn't find a connection."

Lucas grabbed a napkin. "I'll check the FBI's

databases and see if there were other similar cases."

"I'll talk to the detective the sheriff dealt with," Harrison said. "If there's a connection, we might finally get a lead."

HONEY STOPPED BY the ME's office on the way back to her father's house.

"What have you decided to do?" Dr. Weinberger said.

"I haven't," Honey said. "There were no directives in Dad's will and he doesn't own a burial plot. I was thinking about scattering his ashes in the lake or the river."

"You'll have to get permission from the county to do that." Dr. Weinberger gave her the number of the contact person. "There's also a memorial center that has an area specifically designated for urns."

He handed her a couple of business cards from his desk. "How are you holding up?"

Honey offered him a tentative smile. "Fine. Hopefully I'll handle this quickly, then get out of town."

"I'm assuming you'll stay till the sheriff learns who killed your daddy."

Honey leaned against the door. "That depends on how long it takes. I…have jobs waiting on me back in Austin." And people who liked her work and cared about her.

Jared's face flashed through her mind. He was a good friend, trustworthy, and she enjoyed working with him. But she'd never been tempted to kiss him the way she had Harrison.

It would make life simpler if she did want Jared. They made a great team.

She and Harrison had nothing in common except their troubled pasts.

"I'll let you know what I decide to do with the urn," Honey said.

"All right. I'll send his body to the crematorium and they'll call you when it's done."

She thanked the ME then left, her stomach knotting as she passed through town and made her way to Lower Tumbleweed. She parked in the drive, her designer instincts immediately imagining what this house would look like with her touch.

*Don't go there, Honey. You are not taking on this mess.*

The afternoon heat was sweltering and her clothes were sticking to her as she entered the house. She immediately froze, her senses alert as she spotted dishes broken and scattered all over the kitchen counter and floor. The couch cushions had been ripped with a knife, stuffing overflowing and falling out.

Spray paint marred the walls, with a message— Leave Town.

A noise outside startled her, and she gripped her purse, wishing she had her gun. Damn, she'd left it in her nightstand. She rushed down the hall to her room to get it, quickly noting other damage.

The mattress on her father's bed had been ripped, and something red that looked like blood was smeared on the dresser mirror.

Pulse hammering, she dashed into her room. Just as she reached the nightstand and grabbed her gun, the floor squeaked behind her. She started to spin around, but something hard smacked the back of her head.

Pain exploded in her skull, and she swayed. A second later stars swam in front of her eyes then the room blurred into black.

# Chapter Thirteen

Harrison drove back to his office to make the call.

The detective who'd investigated the Waco case was named Jim Hudson. He'd retired five years before.

Harrison spoke with the man's wife, who promised to have him call Harrison. Frustrated, he used a legal pad to list everything he knew so far about Granger and his death.

Granger's murder. The only viable suspect he had at this point was his mother, who had no alibi. But she had no motive to kill Granger now, not after so many years had passed. Unless she'd learned that he had hurt Chrissy. Was it possible that somehow she'd discovered the truth?

If she had, she was so emotional she would have told him or one of his brothers instead of confronting him herself.

Next he wrote Chrissy's name and included everything he'd learned to date about her disappearance. Unfortunately, that wasn't much.

Granger topped the list of suspects, mainly because of the ribbon found at his house. Then Geoffrey Williams. Next he wrote *Chrissy's birth father* with a big question mark beside it.

He made a third column to list anything he learned about this other child so he could make comparisons.

His cell phone beeped. Jim Hudson was returning his call. He introduced himself then explained that he'd spoken to the former sheriff of Tumbleweed. "You worked a case where a little girl went missing two years later, didn't you?"

"Yeah, that case got to me. Never did find the child or figure out who took her."

Harrison rubbed his temple. "Tell me the circumstances."

"Her name was Cady Winters, eight years old. She lived with a single mother who worked at a local hair salon. She left Cady with an elderly grandmother when she was at work."

"Go on."

"The grandmother took her to a local county fair. Said the little girl was there one minute, gone the next. Security searched the fairgrounds and canvassed the workers, but no one had seen her or knew what happened to her."

"The family check out?"

"Yeah, Mom was working. Grandmother's eyesight was failing and she moved slowly, but she adored Cady."

"The father?"

"Died in a car accident the year before. Mother had no boyfriends, no strange neighbors who expressed interest in Cady, no other relatives."

"What about someone at school or their church?"

"They didn't belong to church. I spoke to Cady's teachers and she said Cady was quiet, shy and had very few friends. No one at the school seemed suspicious, either."

"Did you have a theory?" Harrison asked.

Hudson's long-winded sigh rent the air. "I figured it had to be some stranger who saw her at the fair. As much fun as those events are, they're a hunting ground for pedophiles and predators."

"What about the workers?"

"Questioned them all, ran background checks, nothing popped." His voice cracked. "Poor little girl was in the wrong place at the wrong time. Someone lured her away and drove off with her." He paused. "Her name and information is still in the database for the National Center for Missing and Exploited Children"

"Sheriff Dunar told you about my sister?"

"Yes. I suppose the two could be related, but we had no leads to follow."

If Chrissy and this girl had been taken by the same person, they were dealing with a repeat offender.

Possibly a serial kidnapper or killer.

Neither Granger nor Williams fitted that profile.

He thanked the man and asked him to call if he remembered anything else. He hung up then logged on to the computer and ran a search for the girl's name in the NCMEC database.

He drummed his fingers on his desk while he waited. Finally a photo appeared. His stomach convulsed at the image—Cady was blonde and blue-eyed with a big smile that showcased a missing tooth. She looked innocent and sweet just as Chrissy had. She wore a pink flowered jacket, and pink and purple ribbons in her hair and was nuzzling an orange kitten to her cheek.

He was just about to phone Lucas and ask him if he'd found anything regarding the missing Waco girl when his phone buzzed.

He quickly glanced at it—Honey.

Reminding himself to keep it professional, he punched Connect. "Sheriff."

"Harrison…help…"

His heart thundered. "Honey?"

The sound of her labored breathing echoed over the line as he jogged outside to his SUV.

HONEY DRAGGED HERSELF to a sitting position, retrieved her gun and clenched it in her lap in case her attacker returned.

The room spun, and she leaned against her bedroom wall. Her head throbbed. Her fingers met sticky blood in her hair, and she tried to get up, but she had to close her eyes and concentrate to keep from sliding to the floor.

Harrison's voice echoed over the line. "Honey, talk to me. Are you all right?"

Was she? No. "I will be," she murmured.

"I'm on my way." The phone clicked silent, and she let it drop to her lap while she clenched her gun with her other hand. She wouldn't be caught off guard again.

The room blurred. She closed her eyes to stifle the dizziness and inhaled deep breaths. The sound of the wind whipping the trees outside made her tense. She opened her eyes and listened for footsteps. A low clattering sound—mice in the attic?

Seconds slipped into minutes.

Something banged against the house. More rocks? No…a shutter banging in the wind.

It had been windy the day her mother left. When her father told her that her mother was gone, she hadn't thought it would be forever.

Mothers didn't just go away. Even inept ones like hers.

That day Honey had cleaned the house, swept the floors and wiped down the kitchen. She tidied up the living room, made her bed and washed the sheets on her parents' bed. She'd even found an extra pillow in the closet, took a scrap of fabric and made a decorative pillow, thinking her mother would be excited to see things spruced up.

There hadn't been much food in the pantry, but she managed to pull together enough ingredients to make spaghetti and had set the table. She'd fantasized about her parents and her sitting down and having dinner together like a real family.

A tear trickled down her cheek. That hadn't happened.

She'd kept the spaghetti sauce warm for hours,

even after her father had staggered in and passed out on the couch. Hating the rancid way he'd smelled, she'd stepped outside and waited on the porch. Every time a car had driven down the street, she'd hoped it was her mother.

But her mother hadn't come home that night. Or the next or the next.

After a month, she'd stopped listening or watching for her.

She hadn't eaten spaghetti since.

HARRISON ROLLED INTO the Grangers' driveway, senses alert as he scanned the property for trouble. Honey had been here a day and a half and already she'd been vandalized and threatened.

He wouldn't blame her if she packed her bags and left Tumbleweed tonight.

He parked, climbed out, made his way to the porch and knocked. The door wasn't locked, so he eased it open and peered inside.

The living room had obviously been ransacked, couch destroyed and a message painted on the living room wall.

"Honey, it's Harrison." He slowly inched into the hall, praying Honey was okay. The mattress on Waylon Granger's bed had been ripped with a knife, stuffing overflowing, the dresser mirror smeared with something that looked like blood.

"Honey?"

"In here," she called.

He stepped back into the hallway, then toward Honey's room. She staggered toward him and met him in the doorway. He grabbed her arms to steady her. She looked pale, and blood dotted her hair.

"Dammit, Honey, you need a doctor."

"No, just help me so I can wash this blood off."

He slid an arm around her waist and supported her as they walked to the bathroom. "What the hell happened?" he asked.

She sank onto the toilet seat, and he checked her eyes to see if they were clear.

"When I got home, someone had vandalized the place. Whoever it was must have still been here. I hurried to the bedroom to get my gun, but someone struck me from behind."

Just like her father had been hit from behind.

"Let me see where you were hit." Anger mushroomed inside him as she twisted on the seat. He brushed her hair away from the bloody mess. "Good God, Honey. You may need stitches."

"No, I'm fine. Just give me that hand towel."

He snatched one from the towel bar and pressed the towel to her injury to stem the bleeding.

"Did you see who hit you?" Harrison asked.

She shook her head. "No, it happened really quickly." She winced as he removed the towel and examined her wound again.

"You have a gash about an inch long but it's not too deep," Harrison said. "But you could have a concussion, Honey. We should go to the ER."

"I don't need a doctor," she said. "It's just a bump." She took the cloth from him and dabbed it over her injury, cleaning it and the blood from the strands of her golden hair.

"I'm going to call a crime team out here," Harrison said. "Maybe whoever did this left prints."

The message on the wall sounded personal, and in light of the threatening phone call she'd received, he couldn't dismiss the possibility that this person was serious.

And dangerous.

He knelt in front of Honey to check her eyes again. "Are you sure you're all right? Do you feel nauseous?"

"No, I told you I'm fine."

"Maybe you should leave town," Harrison suggested. "I can call you when I solve your father's case."

Honey squared her shoulders. "I'm not leaving, Harrison. I let people run me off when I was young. I won't do it again."

"But this is dangerous, Honey." He gently tucked a strand of her hair behind one ear. "I don't want to see you get hurt."

Her soft whispered sigh tore at him. "Then let's find the answers so we can both put this behind us."

"All right," he conceded. "But you aren't staying here alone. I'll either stay here or you can come to my place."

A sliver of awareness flared in her eyes, then disappeared quickly. Wariness followed.

"Just make the call."

He stood, determined that he would get his way on this.

He didn't intend to let anyone mistreat Honey, not ever again.

HONEY'S FIRST INSTINCT was to clean up the mess her intruder had made, but Harrison reminded her that cleaning would destroy evidence. So she stepped onto the front porch and waited while the crime scene team dusted her house for prints, collected samples of the red smears on the walls and combed the debris from the mattress and couch for a hair or fiber, something that could help identify the culprit.

Needing a distraction from thinking about the attack, she phoned the numbers Dr. Weinberger had given her to discuss the disposal of her father's ashes. A warm breeze blew through, bringing the scent of wildflowers somewhere nearby, and she looked up to see the mountain slopes rising toward the skies at the bluff.

The houses on this street needed to be torn down or gutted, and she'd been so absorbed in the painful memories of her past and her father's murder, that she'd forgotten how beautiful the rugged mountain and terrain was.

Curious as to the status of the other properties,

she phoned a local real estate agent named Isla Fontaine and asked her to find out.

"Most of the properties are owned by the bank," Isla told her.

Harrison stepped outside with the lead crime scene investigator. "We'll analyze the forensics right away," the CSI told Harrison.

"Good. I want to get to the bottom of this," Harrison said.

The crime team left and Honey pocketed her phone. "Thanks for coming, Harrison. I'm going to clean up now."

"I've called a crime scene cleanup team," Harrison said.

"There's no need for that," Honey said. "I can take care of it myself." She started inside but Harrison caught her arm.

"No, you've been through enough today. You need rest."

"I need to have this mess go away," Honey said.

"I understand." Harrison offered her a sympathetic smile. "And it will. But tonight you're coming to my place so you can sleep."

Honey glanced back at the house. The ugly writing on the living room wall mocked her through the screen door.

Harrison was right. She wouldn't be able to sleep in this house tonight.

But staying with Harrison caused anxiety of another kind. It had felt so heavenly when he'd kissed her. She'd felt safe.

And more alive than she'd ever felt in her life.

She wanted that feeling again. To be held in his arms. To have his lips touch hers.

But she was terrified that if he kissed her again, she wouldn't tell him to stop.

## Chapter Fourteen

Harrison's phone buzzed and he quickly connected.

"Harrison," Brayden said, "I talked to Mom about Chrissy's birth father, but she got upset and clammed up."

"Did she tell you the man's name?"

"No, and I don't think she will. She's protecting him for some reason."

Did his mother love the man? If so, why hadn't they gotten together after his father left?

"He may be married, or an affair could mess up his personal life in another way."

Brayden hissed. "Either way, she's not talking. She's adamant that he loved Chrissy and that he would never have hurt her or anyone in our family."

Without knowing the man's identity, Harrison couldn't take his mother's word for it.

Another possibility struck Harrison.

If Chrissy's biological father thought Granger had killed Chrissy, would he have killed Granger to get revenge?

If so, why would he have done so now?

Brayden cleared his throat. "I followed Mom. She's at Reverend Langley's house."

Reverend Langley?

Brayden made a low sound in his throat. "I guess she needed someone to talk to."

Harrison paced the front porch, his heart squeezing at the turmoil on Honey's face. "Maybe."

"What do you want me to do?" Brayden asked.

"Let me handle it. I'm at Honey Granger's right now. Someone broke in, vandalized the place and threatened Honey. I need to get to the bottom of who's doing this."

"You think it has to do with Chrissy?"

"Yes. Either the perp knows Granger did something to Chrissy and killed Granger, or the intruder is afraid Honey is going to find something in her father's house to clear her father and point the finger toward him."

"Let me know if I can do anything else," Brayden said. "I'm going back to the ranch to take care of the horses for the night."

They didn't have livestock at this point, but his mother kept horses so they could ride whenever they wanted.

"Thanks. I'll keep you posted."

Harrison ended the call and pocketed his phone. "Are you ready to go?"

Honey shook her head. "I told you I'm okay to stay alone."

"You are not staying here, Honey, so stop arguing," Harrison said.

A van rolled up, and a man and woman climbed out.

"There's the cleanup crew." Harrison gestured toward the house. "Go pack a bag while I run an errand. I'll come back to get you. You should be safe with them here."

Harrison hurried down the step from the porch, introduced himself to the cleanup crew, then headed to his SUV.

If his mother was talking to the preacher about what had happened, maybe he'd convince her to tell the truth.

Night had fallen, the heat still sweltering. He veered through town then took the side street by the library that led to the church on the outskirts of town. His parents had attended the church together before his father left, then his mother had taken him and his brothers. He searched his memory for any hint of another man his mother had been friendly with, but couldn't recall anyone in particular.

He passed a few cars on the road, but the town seemed quiet tonight. Farmland stretched between the town and the bluff, and the little church sat on a small hill surrounded by open land with the mountains as a backdrop.

The parsonage, a rustic ranch, had been built beside the church for convenience and sat nestled in the woods. The black sedan in the drive belonged to the reverend.

The dark gray SUV was his mother's.

He swallowed hard. She wouldn't be happy to see him or know that Brayden had followed her.

But he didn't intend to let secrets keep him from the truth.

Eighteen years was long enough to live with the lies.

He pulled up the drive and parked, then settled his Stetson on his head as he made his way to the front door.

He raised his fist and knocked, pulse hammering. A minute later the door opened and Reverend Langley greeted him. Silver tipped the reverend's hair, and crow's-feet around his eyes testified to his age.

"Hello, Harrison, I figured you'd show up sometime."

Harrison frowned at his comment. "Can I come in?"

"Of course." He gestured for Harrison to enter, and Harrison stepped inside, then followed the reverend to the den, a cozy room with dark leather furniture and wood floors. A Doberman lay on a braided rug in front of the fireplace.

His mother was perched on the sofa, hands twisting frantically in her lap. "Harrison, what are you doing here?"

"We have to talk," Harrison said.

She stood, arms folded across her chest, her anger a palpable force. For a small-framed woman, she'd never backed down from disciplining her sons, who all stood a foot taller than her. "How did you know where I was?"

Harrison gritted his teeth. "Brayden said you were upset when you left."

"He followed me?" she asked in an incredulous voice.

Harrison shrugged. "He was worried about you."

"I can't believe you and Brayden would follow your own mother," she snapped as if he and Brayden had betrayed her.

"You're the one who lied to us all these years," Harrison said. "And you're still refusing to tell us the truth."

Reverend Langley held up a hand. "Let's all calm down." He gestured to Harrison. "Sit down."

Harrison strode into the living room but leaned against one of the wing chairs that flanked the fireplace. "I'm sorry to intrude on you, Reverend. But I thought my mother might have come to you for advice." He glanced at his mother. "Does he know?"

His mother and the reverend traded an odd look. "Yes," Reverend Langley said.

"Then you know why I'm asking questions about Chrissy's biological father," Harrison said. "He may have something to do with Chrissy's disappearance."

"I told you he didn't," his mother said sharply. "You need to trust me on this, Harrison."

"It's hard to trust someone when you find out they've kept secrets for years, and that they betrayed your father."

"That's enough," Reverend Langley said in a tone that brooked no argument.

His mother started toward the door. "I'm sorry, Ross. I'd better go."

"No." The reverend caught his mother's arm. "It's time to be honest with your boys."

Harrison narrowed his eyes. "He's right, Mother. I'm trying to find out who took Chrissy."

"It wasn't her biological father," the reverend said.

Harrison's look shot to the reverend. "Then you know who took her?"

The man shook his head, his gray eyes serious. "No, but I do know that it wasn't Chrissy's father."

"How do you know that?"

Harrison's mother squeezed the reverend's arm. "Ross, no—"

"It's all right, Ava." Reverend Langley patted his mother's hand then turned to Harrison. "I know Chrissy's birth father didn't hurt her because Chrissy is my daughter and I loved her with all my heart."

HONEY BLINKED BACK tears and hurried to her bedroom as the crime scene team processed the house.

It didn't take Honey five minutes to pack her clothes back in her rolling bag to go to Harrison's. She hadn't exactly unpacked.

Because this house wasn't home.

It was a physical structure where the unhappiness between her parents had affected her. Where love hadn't thrived as it would in a real home, where forgiveness wasn't common, and anger ruled the roost.

If she ever had a family, she would do things differently. Her husband and children would know that she loved them unconditionally.

She froze, one hand gripping the picture of her mother that she'd found. She tried to see her features in her mother, to have some connection, but she felt none.

She stared out at the woods from the porch while the crime scene team worked, a chill washing over her. At five, she'd stood in this same place, gazed out at the woods, and she'd wanted to run away.

Back then she'd been afraid of the dark and spiders and snakes and other creatures that lived in the woods.

Now…she'd renovated so many abandoned, dilapidated houses that critters didn't faze her. She'd grown accustomed to going into a dark house alone at night.

Living alone and sleeping alone meant she didn't have to please anyone or answer to anyone or…be disappointed when they didn't love her back.

She heaved a wary breath.

The only thing that really frightened her now was her crazy attraction to Harrison Hawk.

HARRISON STARED AT the reverend in stunned silence. A quick look at his mother, and guilt streaked her face.

Damn. It had never occurred to him that the man his mother had an affair with was the pastor he'd heard preaching when he was a little boy. The man who'd counseled him on drugs, sex and respecting girls when Harrison was a teenager. The very man who'd taught him to believe in God and to have faith that good prevailed in the end.

Betrayal cut through him. How could he ever look at his mother and this man the same way again?

He held up his hands in disbelief, or maybe it was just that he couldn't handle any more shocking news. He wasn't a kid anymore. He couldn't run from things he didn't want to face or hear.

This was too important.

He wanted, he *needed* to know more.

"I'm sorry, Harrison," Reverend Langley said in the voice he used to soothe agitated parishioners. "It happened a long time ago, right before I decided to give my life to the Lord. In fact, our indiscretion was one reason I decided to serve God."

"You have to understand, Harrison," his mother said in a pleading tone. "We never meant for it to happen. Your father and I were having a difficult time with the ranch, with money, and your father was—"

"Don't make excuses," Harrison said, cutting her off.

"He's right." Reverend Langley patted Harrison's mother's shoulder. "But please know that your mother loved your father dearly, and I respected that. I envied it but I also admired her devotion."

Harrison gave his mother a cutting look. "Devotion would have meant being faithful."

The reverend had the decency to wince. "It was wrong of both of us to betray your father."

"You're damn right it was," Harrison snapped.

"I regretted it the moment it happened," his mother said. "But, Harrison, I never regretted having Chrissy. I loved you boys and I still do. But she was my little girl."

"You're sure she's yours?" he asked the reverend.

The reverend murmured, "Yes. I loved her too much to let her grow up shamed by what we'd done in a moment of weakness." A sad smile settled in his eyes. "I thought she'd be better off raised as a Hawk."

"Are you sure she didn't find out the truth?" Harrison said. "Maybe she heard you and Dad arguing and came to see you that night."

"She didn't hear us," his mother said. "We argued at that stupid party. By the time we got home, we had settled things. Steven knew I loved him and he loved Chrissy and we didn't want to tear her world apart."

"You were okay to stand back and let another man raise your daughter?" Harrison asked the reverend.

"Yes, I told you I loved Chrissy. I wanted what was best for her." Reverend Langley patted the Bible. "I asked for forgiveness and made peace with God and myself a long time ago."

Harrison shifted. The man sounded sincere, like the preacher who'd doled out advice on life to him and his siblings.

Still, the sheriff in him had to ask, "Where were you the night Chrissy disappeared?"

His mother gasped. "Harrison, you can't possibly think—"

Reverend Langley gestured for her to remain calm. "I was attending a private meeting with a pastor in El Paso who offered to mentor me through the seminary. You can check if you need to." He snatched a memo pad from the sofa table, scribbled a name and number, then handed Harrison the paper.

The paper crinkled in Harrison's hand as he stuck it in his pocket. Dammit. He didn't need to call. In spite of his anger, he believed the man.

"My heart has ached every day since Chrissy disappeared," Reverend Langley added softly. "I've prayed you'd find her alive and safe."

Tears blurred Harrison's mother's eyes, and she released a small sob. "When she vanished, I was certain it was God's way of punishing me."

Harrison didn't think God worked like that, but he didn't know what to say. His emotions were all over the place.

His phone buzzed. Lucas.

"I have to go." His mother reached for him, but Harrison wasn't ready to hug and forgive and forget.

"I'll continue to pray you find Chrissy," Reverend Langley said.

Harrison gave him a quick nod, then strode toward the door. He connected the call from Lucas as soon as he stepped outside.

"Yeah?"

"Harrison, I looked into that case you sent me, then checked the FBI databases and there were two other little girls in Texas around the same age who disappeared and were never found."

Harrison's blood ran cold. "You think they're connected?"

A heartbeat passed. "I think it's possible and that we should look into it."

Harrison wiped perspiration from his forehead. If that was true, they were dealing with a serial criminal—perhaps a serial kidnapper/killer.

## Chapter Fifteen

"I'll fax the information on both cases to your office," Lucas said. "Look them over, then we'll interview the families."

"Sounds like a plan." Harrison started his SUV. "I'm just leaving Reverend Langley's house."

"What were you doing there?"

"Brayden followed Mom to the reverend's house. I thought he might convince her to divulge the name of Chrissy's biological father."

"Did he?" Lucas asked.

Harrison silently cursed. "Oh, yeah."

"What does that mean?"

"Chrissy's biological father is the reverend," Harrison said, disgust still eating at him.

"What?" Lucas sounded incredulous. "That can't be right."

"It's not right, but it's the truth," Harrison said. "They both admitted that they slept together when Dad and Mom were having a rough patch."

"My God, I can't believe this," Lucas said with equal parts denial and disapproval.

"According to them," Harrison continued, "they decided Chrissy should grow up in our family as a Hawk."

"Dad knew about this?" Lucas asked.

"Yes, but Mom said she thought they'd gotten

past it. For some reason he brought it up that night at the party, and they argued. I thought Chrissy might have overheard and run off to find her biological father, but Mom insists that Chrissy didn't know she wasn't Dad's."

"Have you told Brayden or Dexter?" Lucas asked.

"Not yet."

"What a mess," Lucas said.

Harrison headed back toward Honey's. "Yeah." It sure was messing with his head.

"I'll talk to Brayden tonight if you'll let Dexter know," Lucas said.

"No problem."

"Just remind Dexter to keep his cool. You know he can be a hothead sometimes."

He rubbed his jaw where he'd borne the brunt of his brother's temper in the past. "I remember," Harrison said. Dexter had been angry when their father left and took that anger out on everyone. Rebellion had fueled his temper, and acting out had been his norm. Their mother had been at her wit's end until a local cowboy/rodeo star had taken Dexter under his wing and taught him to break horses.

But no one had broken Dexter. Even now, instead of conforming to a job where he worked for someone else and had to play by the rules, he'd opened his own detective agency so he didn't have to answer to anyone.

Brayden had been the calm, methodical one, although Harrison always wondered if that tight control wasn't a cover for the anger and hurt beneath the surface.

"Tomorrow let's concentrate on investigating those other two cases. If they're connected," Harrison said, "we might learn something to help solve our own."

Lucas agreed. "It'll go faster if we split up the work. Why don't I talk to the family of the victim from Corpus Christi, and you take the one in Austin?"

"That works for me," Harrison said. "The sooner we question them, the sooner we can get answers."

Although it was past dinnertime and the day was wearing on him, Harrison called Dexter.

Dexter answered on the third ring. "You got news, brother?"

Harrison veered down the street toward Lower Tumbleweed. "I know who fathered Chrissy."

"You mean who Mom cheated on Dad with," Dexter said in a growl.

Harrison gritted his teeth. "Yes. But before I tell you, you have to swear you won't go half-cocked and do something stupid."

"Like what? Pound the bastard's head in?"

"Dexter," Harrison said in a warning voice.

Dexter's dark chuckle rumbled over the line. "I won't do anything you wouldn't do," he said. "Now, spill it. Who is he?"

"Reverend Langley."

His brother took a minute to absorb the information, then Dexter cursed. "Is this some kind of joke?"

"Nope." Harrison paused. "I talked to Mom and him. They confirmed that they were together years ago, but the affair didn't last. Reverend Langley chose to go to the seminary and Mom chose Dad. Dad found out after Chrissy was born."

"But he stayed with Mom after that," Dexter said, confusion lacing his tone.

"Yes. Apparently they agreed not to tell Chrissy and for Dad to raise her as his own."

"Unbelievable."

Harrison silently agreed and parked in the Grangers' drive. The crime scene cleanup crew was still working. "Lucas discovered two cases similar to Chrissy's. We're going to talk to those families tomorrow and compare notes."

An expletive erupted from Dexter. "What can I do to help?"

"Have you been following up with everyone at the bluff that night?" Harrison asked.

"Yeah, but so far nothing. I have a few more names to cross off the list."

"Okay, keep working that angle. Something is bound to break sometime."

Honey stepped onto the porch, and his heart jumped to his throat. She looked so damn beautiful he wanted to haul her in his arms and kiss her.

She was also in danger.

Like it or not, she was stuck with him. There was no way in hell he'd let anyone get to her.

HONEY FORCED A brave smile as Harrison parked.

But the image of those threatening words and the violence in the destruction made her skin crawl. She'd never felt welcome or loved in Tumbleweed, but this intruder was dangerous.

"Just lock up when you leave," Honey told the woman in charge of the cleaning crew. Not that locking up mattered. There was nothing valuable inside, and the vandal had easily broken in.

Harrison stepped from his SUV and she rolled her suitcase to the edge of the porch and handed it to him. He grabbed it while she climbed down the brick step.

She rubbed the back of her head where it was throbbing. Her muscles ached from fatigue and the stress of the day.

"Let's stop and get something to eat on the way to my place."

She sank into the seat, and he drove toward town. His body was stiff, his jaw set tight.

"How did it go with your mother?" she asked softly.

He mumbled something beneath his breath, then explained that he'd met Chrissy's biological father. Then he relayed his conversation with his mother.

"I'm sorry, Harrison. That must have come as a shock."

"Yeah." He turned into the parking lot for the Pie in the Sky, a pizza place that had been built since she'd left town. An outdoor patio offered a view of the mountains and bluff in the distance.

The decor was more eclectic and modern than any place in Tumbleweed, and probably drew the younger crowd as well as families.

Voices and laughter echoed through the open dining area, which was painted blue and silver and boasted scenes of constellations. Country music flowed from an old-fashioned jukebox, and the bar area was packed.

Several teenagers were laughing and hanging out in the back room. The front room held couples, families, and a few truckers occupied a booth to the left. A little boy with dark hair banged his spoon on the table, a mischievous look in his eyes. He reminded Honey of Harrison and what his child might look like.

She froze, wondering where that thought had come from. Then the question—was Harrison involved with anyone? Why wasn't he married?

"It smells good," she commented as the scent of freshly baked pizza wafted toward her from the brick oven.

"Food's good, beer's good," Harrison said as he led her to a booth.

A tall, broad-shouldered man with dark, wavy hair and sparkling green eyes approached them, wiping his hands on an apron. "Nice to have you back, Harrison." The man turned a curious look her way.

"Danny, you remember Honey Granger?" Harrison asked.

"Sure thing. Hey, Honey, I heard you were back." He offered her a big smile. "So sorry about your daddy."

"Thanks."

Harrison angled his head toward her. "Honey, you remember Danny, don't you?"

Her eyes widened. Danny Busby had been a skinny geek in high school with big black square glasses and he'd stuttered. He and Harrison hadn't exactly been friends.

He'd bulked up, the glasses were gone and so was his stutter.

"Of course," she said, finally gathering her wits. "This place looks nice."

He shrugged. "I was a biology major, then decided, what the hell, I always liked to cook so I figured I'd open my own place."

"It's done well," Harrison said. "Just what the town needed."

Danny blushed.

Honey relaxed slightly. The atmosphere was friendlier than the diner where the people had recognized her and hadn't been welcoming.

"What can I get you?" Danny asked.

Harrison ordered a beer and Honey asked for a glass of wine. She needed something to ease the tension from the day. For a moment they discussed what kind of toppings they wanted on their pizza. It seemed surreal, yet normal, almost as if they were on a date.

But this was not a date, and she couldn't harbor false fantasies.

Honey folded the menu and placed it back in the holder on the wall. Harrison did the same, then gripped the beer the waitress delivered and took a sip. His weighted sigh reeked of exhaustion.

But he was still taking care of her.

Emotions welled in her throat. No one had ever done that before.

"How'd it go with the cleaners?" he asked.

She ran a finger along the stem of her wineglass. "Fine. They should be finished soon."

"I'll check with the lab tomorrow to see if they found any forensics." He removed his hat and laid it on the bench seat beside him, then raked a hand through his thick, dark hair. His beard stubble and coppery skin made him look so sexy that she had to tear her gaze away.

"Lucas called," Harrison said in a gruff voice. "There were two other girls around Chrissy's age who went missing after she did."

Honey gasped softly as the implications set in. "You think the same person took them?"

"I don't know, but Lucas and I are investigating the possibility."

He fell silent as the pizza arrived, and Honey contemplated the implications of his discovery.

If he was right, that meant a serial kidnapper/killer had been preying on little girls. A serial criminal who might live in Tumbleweed.

## Chapter Sixteen

Honey felt as if everyone in the restaurant was looking at her, but when she glanced around, she realized she was being paranoid.

Old habits died hard.

Not everyone in Tumbleweed remembered her, especially the younger generation.

She offered to help pay the bill, but Harrison insisted on taking care of it. Tension knotted her shoulders as they climbed into his SUV.

It hadn't occurred to her that staying at Harrison's might mean his family ranch. "Do you still live at Hawk's Landing?" she asked. If he did, she'd insist on a motel.

"Not at the main house," he said. "We had some cabins built on the property for workers when my dad used to raise cattle, so I moved into one of them for more privacy. Since I became sheriff and my brothers have their own lives and jobs, we got out of the cattle business. We keep a few horses for riding."

"Do your brothers still live at home?"

He shook his head. "Like me, they wanted their own places, so each of us took a cabin. Although Lucas is with the FBI and has a place in San Antonio. Brayden works for a law firm in Austin and has a loft downtown."

"And Dexter?"

"He has a PI office in Tumbleweed and an apartment in Austin, as well."

She relaxed slightly, grateful she didn't have to face Harrison's family tonight. He turned onto the oak-lined drive into Hawk's Landing, and Honey's heart stuttered. She had heard things in town about how beautiful the ranch was but the descriptions didn't do it justice.

Acres and acres of plush green grass spread before her. The land was flat at first but gave way to rolling hills leading into the mountains. He drove past the main farmhouse, a sprawling white two-story, showcasing wraparound porches complete with rocking chairs and a porch swing. A stable and riding pen sat adjacent to the house, and several horses galloped freely on a hill in the distance.

"I heard your ranch was beautiful, but this is amazing," she said in awe. "Do you miss ranching?"

Harrison shrugged, his jaw tight. "Sometimes. I loved it as a kid when my dad was here, but it's hard work. And after Chrissy disappeared, all I did was think about finding her killer."

"That's the reason you went into law enforcement," Honey said more as a statement than a question.

He nodded. "Yeah."

"And your brothers followed suit?"

"I guess they were driven for the same reasons I was." He shrugged, the SUV bouncing over the graveled drive. "My mother was disappointed that we didn't keep up the cattle business, but she understood. She wanted answers, too."

"Of course you all did."

His gaze met hers as he parked in front of a small log cabin, which backed up to the creek. For a moment, tension lingered between them then she followed him inside.

The rustic furnishings were masculine but homey. On the mantel, a family picture caught her eye and made her feel totally out of place.

She didn't belong here in Tumbleweed, especially at Harrison Hawk's house. Another photo of Chrissy that must have been taken shortly before she went missing sat beside the family picture. In the photo, she was wearing the yellow ribbons. He paused to look at it and Honey couldn't resist. She took his hand in hers. His was big, strong, wide with long fingers while her hand seemed tiny next to his.

Unlike most women he probably dated, her nails were filed short and blunt, her hands rough from refurbishing houses.

His eyes darkened as he looked at her hand. He licked his lips.

Dear heavens, she wanted to kiss him.

"We're getting close," she said softly. "I can feel it."

Another hesitation, and she realized she was talking as much about them as she was about finding out the truth about Chrissy.

She wanted to be closer.

A dark, primal hunger radiated from his eyes, and she sensed he wanted more, too. That he was hurting and confused and needed comfort as much as she did.

She squeezed his hand and leaned toward him. He took her face in his and stared deep into her eyes.

Hunger and desire spiraled in her belly, and she sighed softly, letting him know that she wanted him.

His gaze raked over her, but he resisted. For a fraction of a second.

Then he drew her into his arms and closed his mouth over hers. She gave in to the moment and the heat simmering between them and slipped her hands around his neck. He felt warm and strong and hungry, a potent combination that stirred her own primal desires.

He plunged his tongue into her mouth, and she opened and welcomed him, meeting his urgency with her own as she dragged her hands across his back. She wanted to touch him and taste him, to feel him naked and hot, bare skin to bare skin.

She'd never wanted a man like that.

It scared her to think that she did now.

His family hated her. Or at least his mother did.

His hands trailed down her back to her hips, and she moaned as he deepened the kiss. Her body hummed with desire, overruling her common sense, and she pulled at his shirt and opened the top two buttons so she could slip her hands inside and touch his bare skin.

Heaven. It was pure heaven feeling the heat emanating from him, and knowing that he wanted her.

That touching her was exciting him.

She groaned and he yanked her closer, pressing his thick length against her belly so his erection pulsed between her legs. Raw need pummeled her.

She'd only been with a couple of men in the past, and no one who rivaled Harrison in the sex appeal department. No one she'd liked and admired and felt such a connection to.

No one she'd loved...

Her heart hammered. Her pulse stopped. She froze, cold fear gripping her in a vise.

Loved?

She'd never loved a man in her life. Had never even wanted to be in a long-term relationship.

She'd only meant to survive.

First as a child with her parents' dysfunction and then the stigma of the gossip in Tumbleweed. The past few years she'd poured herself into her job, building a career and a name for herself.

She'd been on her own.

She didn't know how to be anything else.

Harrison groaned and planted kisses along her neck, and she clung to him, wanting him to take her to bed.

But if he did that, she'd be lost to him forever.

And she could not lose herself.

She was the only person she could count on. For God's sake, she'd learned that at a young age. She was simply feeling weak because she was back in Tumbleweed.

He kissed her again, and she kissed him back, but slowly ended the kiss and pulled away.

"We can't do this," she whispered, remembering his mother's animosity.

He lowered his head, tilted his forehead against hers, his breathing ragged as they held each other and the heat slowly cooled between them.

"I should go to bed," she whispered.

He nodded but instead of releasing her, one hand brushed her breast as he lifted it to her chin. "I'll show you the way."

God, she wanted that.

She barely bit back a moan and fought her instincts to drag him to bed with her. It would feel so good to be naked in his arms, to have him inside her, to hear him calling her name in the throes of passion.

A weary breath escaped her. That could never be. Girls like her didn't end up with men like Harrison Hawk.

She gave him a gentle push, silently telling him they had to stop this craziness, and he stepped back.

Turmoil darkened his eyes, desire and regret blending, then he raked a hand through his hair and released her. "The guest room's this way."

She couldn't bring herself to speak so she simply nodded, then followed him to a second bedroom, which thankfully had its own bath. A log cabin quilt draped a four-poster bed with a painting of Hawk's Landing centered above the bed.

The painting was a reminder of where she was and the family who owned the land and this cabin. Of the son who had gone into law enforcement to solve his sister's case.

"What's going to happen tomorrow?" she asked.

He paused, his shoulders rigid. When he turned back to face her, he wore his sheriff's expression.

"I'm going to Austin to interview the family of one of the victims," he said gruffly. "I won't rest until the bastard who took Chrissy is behind bars."

Or dead, she thought, sensing his underlying meaning as he stalked to his bedroom and closed the door.

Body still humming with unspent passion, she stripped her clothes and dragged on pajamas.

But as she climbed into bed, she closed her eyes and imagined Harrison crawling in beside her, naked and hot with need.

Her body tingled with desire as she envisioned him above her, his arms braced as he thrust inside her, his eyes hooded with passion meant for her.

One touch of his lips and they'd forget the reasons they shouldn't be together, and they'd make love until dawn.

WHAT THE HELL was wrong with him?

Why couldn't he keep his hands off Honey?

Harrison retreated to his bedroom, disgusted with

himself. Thank God she'd had the good sense to stop things or right now he'd be naked in the bed with her, feasting on her body and tasting every inch of her.

He flipped the shower water to cold, stripped and dived beneath the spray, desperately needing to wrangle his libido under control.

He hadn't felt like this with a woman in ages. Maybe never.

Truthfully, though, he hadn't dated much. He'd been too focused on his family and his sister's case to pursue a relationship with anyone.

Why Honey, though? And why now?

Because their emotions were running high from the threats against her and the connection between their families?

He closed his eyes and willed away images of Honey's golden hair spread across his pillow. Of her lips on his. Of her body joining his in blissful pleasure.

Despite the cold water, his traitorous body wanted her.

Dammit.

He finally shut off the shower, dried off, dragged on boxers and padded his way to the bed.

But when he lay down, more images of Honey came to him.

She was in the next room, probably curled up in his guest bed asleep. Was she wearing some skimpy nightgown? Or was she naked?

Was she still thinking of him?

He punched his pillow and rolled to his stomach. It didn't matter. He couldn't have her. Not even once.

If he did, he'd want her again. And again.

Her big, sad eyes haunted him.

Tomorrow he had work to do. She was right— they were uncovering the truth about his sister.

Trouble was, he was getting closer to Honey, too.

But he had to stay focused.

He closed his eyes, and this time he pictured his little sister in his mind. If she'd lived, she might be married by now. Might have a family.

Hell, all of their lives would be different. His parents might have stayed together.

And he…he didn't know what he'd be doing. If he would have become sheriff or if he might have taken over the ranch.

But it did no good to think of "what if."

He was mired in reality. His family had lived in the dark for years. Guessing and imagining the worst. Hoping and praying for the best.

Struggling through each Christmas and birthday with a hole in their hearts.

And nothing could change that.

# Chapter Seventeen

Harrison barely slept. Keeping his body in his own bed had consumed all his energy.

He took another shower to wake himself up, then dressed and brewed a pot of coffee. By the time Honey emerged from the bedroom dressed and showered, he'd cooked bacon, eggs and toast.

She looked surprised to see food on the table. "You didn't have to make breakfast."

"I needed food," he said. He'd had to stay busy to distract himself from joining her in the damn shower.

She looked wary but sank into a chair and sipped the coffee he poured for her. He claimed the chair across from her and wolfed down his food, anxious to get on the road. Being in close quarters with Honey was too damn tempting.

She buttered her toast then added jelly and took small bites in silence.

"Did you sleep okay?" he finally asked.

Her gaze met his. "Yes. Thanks for letting me stay here. I'm sure I got more sleep than I would have at my dad's."

He wiped his mouth. "Have you decided what you're going to do with his house?"

She sipped her coffee. "I've spoken to the local real estate agent about the neighborhood. Some of the houses already belong to the bank so an investor could pick them up for a good price and build a nice group of homes."

"That would be good for the town," Harrison said as he grabbed another piece of toast.

"The trouble is people need jobs, and Tumbleweed doesn't look as if it's grown since I left."

"True. We need something to draw people," he said, although he had no answers for the economy. His job was to protect the citizens.

He carried his plate to the sink, rinsed it and put it in the dishwasher. "I'm going to Austin this morning to talk to the family of one of the girls who went missing. You're welcome to stay here or I can give you a ride back to your father's house to retrieve your car."

"Let me go with you to Austin," Honey said. "I need to check on a project I have there."

"Can't you handle that over the phone?"

"I could, but it would be nice to get away from Tumbleweed for a little while."

He understood. Things had been intense.

"I like to review the details of the design myself, too." She cleaned her plate and rinsed her coffee cup while he strapped on his gun and holster. Being in his kitchen and sharing breakfast with her felt too intimate and made him wonder what it would be like if they had made love and then shared breakfast.

Dangerous thoughts.

He stepped outside for air while she grabbed her purse and phone. They drove to Austin in silence, the miles ticking away as the ranches and farmland grew more sparse and the city slipped into view.

He'd already phoned the family to ask if he could stop by so he drove to their house first.

"Tell me about these people," Honey said as he parked.

He killed the engine. "Their names are Irene and Karl Armond. Their daughter Yvonne disappeared about six months after Chrissy did. No one has heard from her or seen her since."

"My father never drove as far as Austin," Honey said. "And if these two cases are connected that means someone was preying on young girls back then."

Harrison nodded. "Exactly. We might be dealing with a serial predator."

HONEY FIDGETED AS she got out of the SUV.

If that was true, they might prove her father was innocent. But it also meant that Sheriff Dunar had missed something.

"You said there were two girls?" Honey said as they walked up the drive.

Harrison nodded. "Lucas is going to talk to the other family."

The Armonds lived in an overgrown ranch house outside Austin in a small neighborhood that looked family friendly. A blue sedan sat in the drive, a pickup behind it.

Harrison knocked on the door, and footsteps sounded inside, then a female voice yelled to hold on.

"Did they have other children?" Honey asked.

Harrison nodded. "An older daughter. I'm not sure what happened to her."

The door opened, and a fiftysomething woman with a thick, silver-streaked bob answered the door. A tall thin man with hunched shoulders stood behind her, puffing on a cigarette.

Harrison identified himself, then Honey. "May we come in?"

"I don't know how we can help you," Mr. Armond said.

"I just need a few minutes." Harrison brushed past the woman, and Honey followed.

The house was outdated with worn linoleum, yellowing tile, and smelled of dog. She spotted food and water bowls at the edge of the laundry room, then saw a big, furry animal sprawled on a towel in the kitchen.

"You want coffee?" Mrs. Armond asked.

Harrison declined, and Honey thanked her but shook her head. The woman led them to the den, where a plaid couch and recliner flanked the fireplace.

They took seats and Mr. Armond stubbed his

cigarette out in the ashtray. "Do you have new information about Yvonne?"

Harrison's jaw tightened. "I'm afraid not," he said. "But my sister disappeared from the small town of Tumbleweed a few months before your daughter went missing. I'm still working her case. It's possible the two are connected."

Mrs. Armond's eyes widened. "You think the same person kidnapped them?"

"I'm not sure, but answering my questions could help us both."

Mr. Armond rubbed the back of his neck with a groan. "Do we have to drag this up again?" Pain underscored his tone. "Every time we do, Irene doesn't sleep for weeks. We get our hopes up and then get all disappointed again. We can't take it anymore."

"I'm so sorry," Harrison said. "I understand how you feel. My family and I have suffered the same way."

Mrs. Armond twisted her hands in her lap. Honey stroked one freckled hand to calm her twitching. "Trust me, he wants to help."

Mr. Armond started to speak again, but his wife pressed her hand over his. "Let's talk to him. Maybe this time we'll get some answers. If we find our baby, we can finally put her to rest and she'll be at peace."

"WHAT DO YOU want to know?" Mrs. Armond asked.

Harrison knew damn well how difficult it was

sitting in this couple's shoes, being questioned by the police, at the same time wondering if the people were trying to pin the crime on you.

"Tell us about the day your daughter went missing, and the days before. Sometimes we remember things after time passes that can help." He gave the couple an understanding smile. "Even if my sister's disappearance isn't related, fresh eyes and ears can pick up things that others missed."

She nodded, and she and her husband grasped hands. Comforting to see that even though they'd lost a child, it hadn't completely broken them apart as it had his parents.

Then again...his mother's affair and Chrissy's paternity had been a double-edged sword.

Mr. Armond removed another cigarette and rolled it between his fingers. "Yvonne was ten years old," he said in a voice that sounded far away, as if he was literally traveling back in time. "She liked softball, climbing trees and animals."

Harrison smiled, his heart aching. "My sister was a tomboy, too. Of course, she had to be. She had four brothers."

The couple shared a soft laugh. "I imagine so," Mrs. Armond said. "Our other daughter, Hazel, is the opposite. Such a girlie girl."

"Did they get along?" Honey asked.

Mrs. Armond fidgeted again. "Most of the time. Hazel tried to get Yvonne interested in girlie things like pretty clothes and lipstick and hair ribbons."

"Ribbons?" Harrison said, the memory of Chrissy playing with the ribbons in her treasure box taunting him.

Mrs. Armond nodded. "Hazel spent her allowance at the sale rack, buying ribbon by the yard. She tied them around her ponytail, and she learned how to make bows and hot glued them to barrettes."

Mr. Armond leaned forward, then dropped the cigarette onto the coffee table. "Is that important?"

Harrison exhaled slowly. "It might be." He paused. "Go on."

"Yvonne had a lot of friends in school," Mrs. Armond continued. "She played soccer and liked mystery books, and she loved animals, especially horses. We used to have an old mare that she rode. She loved rodeos so much that for her birthday, we got tickets…"

"God, I regret that," Mr. Armond said.

Honey stiffened, but Harrison forced himself not to react. "She disappeared at the rodeo?"

Yvonne's mother clung to her husband's hand. "Yes."

"If we'd stayed home that day, Yvonne might still be with us," Mr. Armond choked out.

"I'm so sorry," Honey said softly. "But it's not your fault. You loved her and wanted to make her happy."

Anguish wrenched the woman's face as she wiped at fresh tears.

"Tell me about that day," Harrison said. "Did your other daughter go with you?"

Mrs. Armond nodded. "Yes. She wanted to stay home with her boyfriend, but we insisted it was a family event and we were celebrating Yvonne's birthday." She paused, sweat beading her forehead.

"Her boyfriend showed up," Mr. Armond continued. "Hazel slipped off to meet him and left Yvonne alone at the concession stand."

Harrison's stomach churned. "That's when she went missing?" he asked softly.

The couple both nodded, grief emanating from them.

Harrison forced his voice to remain calm, nonjudgmental. "Did Hazel see anyone watching Yvonne or paying attention to her?"

"No," Mr. Armond said with a slight tinge of bitterness. "She said Yvonne went to get a snow cone. She was infatuated with the balloons. Hazel figured she just wandered off. So she went to make out with this guy while her sister was taken."

Harrison gritted his teeth. The scenario could have fitted a hundred child abductions.

If a predator was hunting, watching for an opportunity, he pounced when given one.

"How old was Hazel at the time?" he asked.

Mrs. Armond wiped at her eyes again. "Fourteen."

"She blamed herself," Mr. Armond said. "She

went into a depression, and for a while we thought we'd lost her, too."

"We were so distraught ourselves that we were rough on her at first," Mr. Armond added grimly.

"But we went to counseling," Mrs. Armond added. "We realized that Hazel was just a kid and we forgave her."

"Did she forgive herself?" Harrison asked.

The woman shook her head sadly. "I don't think so. She works with troubled kids now through a YMCA."

Harrison felt a kinship with Hazel. "Is there anything else you can think of about that day? Did you see strangers, perhaps a vendor or rodeo worker watching your daughter?"

They both looked lost, as if they were struggling for details.

"There was a group of mentally challenged and handicapped children there." Mrs. Armond stroked the chain of her necklace, then rubbed her fingers over a chip attached to the end. A sobriety chip from AA. "She talked to all of those kids."

"She talked to a teenager mucking the stalls, too," Mr. Armond said. "But the sheriff questioned him and he was cleared."

Frustration gnawed at Harrison. He'd hoped to get a concrete suspect, but just as the sheriff's report stated, they hadn't narrowed down one.

Still, their conversation confirmed that the cases

might be connected. That a serial predator had been hunting in Texas for years.

It was high time someone stopped him.

# Chapter Eighteen

"Did detectives question people at the rodeo?" Harrison asked.

"Yes," Mr. Armond said. "One lady saw Yvonne talking to a rodeo clown. A teenager claimed she saw her at the cotton candy stand."

"Were there security cameras?"

Mr. Armond shook his head. "Not back then."

Damn, that would have helped.

"You never received a ransom note or message of any kind?" Harrison asked.

"No." Mrs. Armond's voice broke. "Not that we had any money, but we would have done everything possible to raise some if we'd received a note."

Harrison cleared his throat. "Did Yvonne have anything with her when she was taken?"

"What do you mean?" Mr. Armond asked.

"Like a backpack or toy?"

"She liked real horses but she was obsessed with unicorns," Mrs. Armond said. "We gave her a stuffed one for her birthday. She had it with her that day."

"Was it recovered after she disappeared?" Harrison asked.

"No." Mrs. Armond picked up a photo book from the coffee table, flipped through the pages and showed them a picture of Yvonne wearing a birthday hat and hugging the colorful unicorn.

One of Mrs. Armond's teardrops fell on the picture book. "Before we went to the rodeo, she braided the unicorn's mane and tied it with ribbons."

Mr. Armond curved his arm around his wife and pulled her against him in a comforting gesture.

"I hoped we'd find it and it would lead us to Yvonne, but the longer she was gone, I just prayed she had it with her. It would have given her comfort."

Harrison hissed a breath. "Could I see her room?"

Mrs. Armond stood slowly. Her husband snatched the cigarette and lit it.

He and Honey followed Mrs. Armond down the hall past the master bedroom to the room on the end. "I haven't changed a thing since we lost her. I kept hoping she'd come back and..."

Pick up where they'd left off.

"My mother kept my sister's room just as she'd left it, too," he said, his throat thickening.

Mrs. Armond gave him a knowing smile, obviously grateful he understood. Like his family, so many people told them they needed to move on. Pack up Chrissy's things and give them away. Turn her room into a guest room or a media room or office.

But doing that meant forgetting about her, erasing her from their lives as if she never existed.

That was something he and his family could never do.

HONEY'S HEART ACHED for this couple. Just like the Hawks, their lives had been torn apart by the loss of a child.

How did one overcome such a tragedy? Parents weren't supposed to bury their children. It should be the other way around.

Harrison looked solemn as they entered Yvonne's room. A pink ruffled bedspread with matching curtains added a feminine touch, although the bookcase held plastic toy ponies and a framed photograph of Yvonne playing T-ball.

Children's books lined the shelves as well, and a jewelry box took center stage. Harrison tugged on latex gloves and opened the box, revealing an assortment of plastic necklaces, beads and rings. A wooden doll with braids made of yarn held an assortment of colorful bows.

Harrison used his phone to snap pictures of the room and items inside. True to Mrs. Armond's words, the little girl's clothes still hung in the closet. A bright pink jacket hung next to a pink cowboy hat. Cowboy boots, sneakers and black patent leather shoes lined the shoe shelf.

Tears blurred Honey's eyes. The furniture looked polished as if the Armonds kept it clean, just waiting for Yvonne's return.

Harrison rifled through school notebooks on the child's desk. Honey spotted a diary, picked it up and skimmed several entries. Typical ten-year-old comments about her friends at school, the horse she wanted her parents to buy for her at the stable where she rode, and a boy at the stables who annoyed her because he pulled her pigtails.

Honey smiled. Two years later and she probably would have had a crush on the kid.

"I don't see anything helpful," Harrison said. "I'm going to request a copy of the file on the investigation. Maybe the detective mentioned a similarity to Chrissy's case."

"Maybe." Although so far, nothing had stuck out.

The Armonds were standing at the door waiting, a wistful sadness emanating from them.

"Please let us know if you learn anything," Mr. Armond said.

Harrison promised he would, then Honey followed him outside.

"What do you think?" Honey asked as they got in the SUV.

"The only commonality so far is the age of the girls and that they both liked ribbons in their hair. But most little girls do."

"That's true," Honey agreed.

"Yvonne disappeared from a public event, the rodeo, where strangers as well as numerous workers and cowboys were in attendance."

"Still, no one saw anything," Honey said. "If someone wanted to kidnap her, he could have lured her away with a toy, balloons, even a rodeo animal."

"But Chrissy disappeared from the bluff where a bunch of teenagers were hanging out. Unless one of them also attended the rodeo, I don't see how we're dealing with the same perp."

"Did you suspect anyone at the bluff?" Honey asked.

Harrison drummed his fingers on the steering wheel as he pulled from the drive. "My brother mentioned that one of his friends shoved Chrissy that night. Geoffrey Williams."

Harrison snatched his phone and punched a number. "Lucas, I just talked to the Armonds. Their daughter disappeared from a rodeo. Check and see if Geoffrey Williams attended that rodeo."

A hesitation. "Okay, thanks. Let me know what you learn from the Ritter family."

He ended the call and rolled his shoulders. "You wanted to check on one of your projects. Which way?"

Honey directed him toward the neighborhood south of Austin where her latest renovation was underway.

She wondered what Harrison would think of her work. For some reason, she wanted to show him that she'd risen above her white trash roots and made something of herself.

HARRISON WOVE THROUGH the streets of Austin, his heart hammering. He sensed he was onto something with the case, but he wasn't sure what it was.

Traffic sounds, cars honking, people bustling on

the sidewalk, everyone in a hurry… City life. It was quitting time already, and happy hour had begun.

The restaurants were crowded, music blaring from bars, city lights twinkling, the sidewalks packed with residents and tourists.

So different from Tumbleweed and the quiet countryside, the slower pace, the ranches and farm animals, the friendly faces.

Except someone in Tumbleweed might have been hiding behind a friendly face for years. His sister's kidnapper/killer could have been living in town laughing at him as sheriff because he hadn't put together the pieces of the puzzle to unearth the truth.

"It's the neighborhood on Silver Spurs Drive," Honey said. "Turn left at that next light and take it about five miles."

He made the turn, grateful to be leaving the heart of the city and driving into the less crowded neighborhoods that fanned out from Austin. He passed a new condo development complete with offices, businesses and restaurants then an apartment community and another business development.

Three miles later Honey pointed to another turn. Although they were within ten miles of the city, it felt as if he was driving into the wilderness.

"This is an older development," Honey said. "Most of the houses are in disrepair, but I bought a couple to flip."

"How did you get into the business?"

Honey's face seemed to change as he entered the

neighborhood. Her eyes looked brighter, hopeful, void of the pain and emptiness that haunted her in Tumbleweed.

"It's kind of a long story," she said.

"We've got time."

Honey squared her shoulders. "After I left Tumbleweed, I got a job as a waitress and rented a room from this lady. Her house was falling apart, so in my spare time, I helped fix it up. It took a couple of years, but the house came alive."

"Sounds like you found your calling," Harrison said.

Honey shrugged. "I enjoyed taking something that was in ruins and fixing it. The woman and her family liked the changes. When she died, her son, a general contractor, was so impressed with the improvements, that he offered me a job as his designer. I took some classes on the side and we've done okay."

"We're working on that ranch right now," she said as they bypassed two other houses that looked as if they needed her touch. Work crews were all over the yard and ranch house.

He pulled in the driveway and parked, and Honey slid from the SUV. "I won't be long, but if you have something else you need to do, I can get a ride and meet you."

His pulse jumped as a tall dark-haired guy in jeans and a work shirt loped out, a tool belt around his hips. The man swept Honey into a big bear hug.

No wonder she'd put the brakes on the night before when he'd kissed her. She obviously had someone waiting on her here in Austin.

HONEY GAVE JARED a hug, grateful for his support and for picking up the slack in her absence.

"You okay?" he asked.

She nodded, puzzled by the scowl on Harrison's face. "I should have things tied up soon and be back."

Harrison's jaw tightened, and she introduced him to Jared.

"Jared is the contractor I told you about," she said. "He's been manning the crew while I was gone." She motioned to the house. "Let me take a quick look around, then we'll go."

"Are you going to give me the tour?" Harrison asked.

If there was one thing Honey enjoyed, it was showing off her reno projects. "Sure." She turned to Jared. "Anything I need to know about?"

He shrugged. "We had a delay with the cabinets, but we're back on track now. We'll be cutting it close to the deadline, but we should make it."

"Great." Her heart stuttered as she led Harrison into the house. "We replaced old linoleum with hardwood floors throughout," she said to give him an idea of just how much the house had changed. "Luckily we found shiplap in the den and dining room so we restored that and rebricked the fireplace." She paused at the kitchen. "The house was cut into choppy rooms, but we took out walls and reconfigured the space to create an open concept between the kitchen, dining and living areas. A local woodworker custom built a farm table and bench to fit the house."

From the kitchen, she showed him a powder room that had been redesigned, then the master bedroom with a vaulted ceiling and a massive bathroom. The tile work in the shower was intricate, the cabinets and counter were reflective of the farmhouse style she'd chosen in the other room.

Harrison scanned each room, a smile twitching at his face. "The house is stunning," he said. "You're obviously good at what you do."

Honey's throat closed. Jared had praised her work and so had a few Realtors and clients, but hearing the admiration in Harrison's voice touched her deeply.

The people in Austin didn't know about her past or her family or the names the kids had called her. She'd left that behind when she'd run from Tumbleweed.

Although returning to the small town had resurrected those memories. But she wouldn't be staying there.

Her life was here.

And Harrison's was back in the town near his family. With his mother, the woman who hated her.

HARRISON WAS IMPRESSED with Honey's work. She changed when she spoke of the house and design.

But on the way back to Tumbleweed, she lapsed into a tense silence. They stopped at a barbecue restaurant and ate, the tension still thick between them.

She was probably thinking about Jared, maybe missing him. Counting the days until she would be with him again, back doing the work she loved.

It was where she belonged.

Clouds rolled in, darkening the sky as he headed along the interstate. He hoped to hear back from Lucas, but the miles stretched out without a call. By the time they made it to Tumbleweed, Honey was fidgeting, agitated.

"Why don't you drop me off at my father's? I can stay there tonight."

Harrison chewed the inside of his cheek. "It's not safe," he said. "You're staying at my place."

She bit her bottom lip and glanced ahead, and he wondered if she was nervous.

"Listen, Honey, I promise I'll leave you alone. I won't kiss you or push myself on you again."

Her eyes widened, and she opened her mouth to speak, but looked down at her hands then ahead again.

Harrison spotted a bright light ahead. A light coming from lower Tumbleweed. "Good God, Honey." He accelerated and flipped on his siren. "Call 911."

Honey fumbled as she punched the numbers on her cell phone. "It's my father's neighborhood," she cried. "Hurry, Harrison. There's a fire!"

# *Chapter Nineteen*

Honey gave the address to the 911 operator. "Please hurry," she said as Harrison rounded the corner and turned onto her street. Flames shot into the sky, smoke billowing in a thick cloud.

The back side of her father's house was engulfed. Flames ate at the dry grass, spreading to the two neighboring houses. The wind picked up, blowing smoke so thick that as Harrison parked and she threw the door open, she could hardly see the driveway.

Her feet crunched gravel, though, as she dropped to the ground.

"Stay in the SUV!" Harrison shouted.

But panic seized Honey and his words sounded as if they'd come from far away. She had to get her mother's picture.

Heart hammering, she ran toward the front of the house and darted inside. Heat seared her and smoke clogged her lungs.

"Honey, stop!" Harrison yelled behind her.

But Honey plunged on. There wasn't much inside she wanted to save, but the picture she'd found was the only one she had of her mother. She coughed, feeling her way through the smoke until she found it, then dashed down the hall to her room to retrieve the jewelry box. If she ever had a little girl, she wanted to pass it on.

Fire snapped and wood crackled and popped as flames engulfed the back walls and room. The flames had inched into her room and were climbing the wall, quickly feeding on the battered wood and rotting boards. The jewelry box was sitting atop her old dresser, which had started to catch fire.

She grabbed a bathroom towel, then wrapped it around her hand as she reached for the jewelry box.

"What the hell are you doing?" Harrison yanked her back toward the door.

"Let me go!" she shouted.

"The roof is going to give any second!"

She pushed at his hands. "Let me go. I want my jewelry box."

He cursed. "Dammit, Honey, it's not worth it!"

"It's all I've got left." Tears blurred her eyes. She hadn't realized how important it was that she keep something from her childhood, but now she did.

She started back into the bedroom, but he caught her arm. "I'll get it. Stay here!"

He took the towel, pushed ahead of her and darted through the rising flames. The wall in the back collapsed with a crash, the ceiling raining down flaming boards. Sparks flew and heat seared her.

A crashing sound echoed through the house, roaring with the noise of wood cracking, and she shouted Harrison's name.

If he got hurt, she'd never forgive herself.

She stepped toward her bedroom, but flames engulfed her old bed. "Harrison!"

Panic nearly crippled her as she searched the smoky haze for him.

It seemed like an eternity, but finally he grabbed her hand. "We have to get out of here now!" He tucked the jewelry box under one arm, and the two of them ran through the house. Wood splintered and windows shattered. They dodged fiery debris and jumped over patches of flames eating the rotting floor.

She coughed and clung to Harrison's hand as they ducked to avoid a falling board. She shouldn't have let Harrison risk his life to save her childhood jewelry box. There wasn't anything valuable inside, no precious gems or antiques or family heirlooms.

Just cheap beads and bracelets she'd played with as a kid, ones that had belonged to her mother.

A loud boom sounded and the roof collapsed. Sparks flew and pummeled them as they ran onto the porch, then jumped to the ground and raced to safety.

HARRISON COVERED HONEY'S head to protect her from being hit by flying embers as they dived beneath a live oak. The sound of glass shattering and wood crashing down splintered the air.

Granger's house was totally engulfed in flames, the two houses nearest it smoking and burning, as well.

A siren wailed. Brakes squealed as the fire engine careened into the drive.

He quickly searched Honey's face. "Are you okay?"

She nodded. "Thanks for saving my jewelry box."

"You're welcome." He pushed himself up. He had no idea what was so valuable inside, but it had been important to Honey, so he'd had to retrieve it.

"Let me talk to the firefighters." Harrison jogged to the fire engine to meet the rescue workers. A big, burly man named Wes Comber introduced himself as the fire chief.

"The first house is a goner," Harrison said to the chief, referring to the Grangers' home. "I doubt you can save the other two, but we need to contain the fire so it doesn't spread to the woods."

The chief shouted orders to his team and they quickly began to work, unrolling the hoses and aiming the spray on the ground by the other houses, then the houses themselves to keep the fire contained.

"What happened?" the chief asked.

Harrison shrugged. "I don't know." He pointed toward Honey. "Miss Granger's father owned the house that was engulfed when you arrived. We were in Austin today. When we got here, everything was ablaze."

"These houses are old," the chief said. "You think she lit a candle and left it, or used the stove and there was faulty wiring?"

"I think there's foul play. Miss Granger's father was murdered a few days ago, and since she returned to Tumbleweed, she's been threatened and attacked."

Deep frown lines marred the man's face as he studied the blaze. "I'll have my men look for point of origin and evidence of arson."

"Thanks." Cold fear seized Harrison. What if the perpetrator had set the fire while Honey was inside?

She could have been hurt or…worse. Killed.

The thought of something happening to her made anger churn in his gut. It wouldn't happen…not on his watch.

HONEY WIPED SWEAT and soot from her forehead as her childhood home crumbled to the ground.

If there had been any happy memories in that house, they'd died years ago, destroyed by the misery of living with her father and knowing her mother hadn't loved her enough to stay around.

The embers burned bright against the brittle grass, orange and yellow glowing in the dark. Thankfully the homes were vacant so no one was inside or hurt.

The firemen worked diligently to extinguish the blaze over the next two hours. Wildfires could be dangerous and run rampant, destroying miles of woods and homes if left untended in these dry conditions. Just last year fourteen people had died in a wildfire accidentally set by teenagers when their campfire got out of control.

Harrison coordinated with the firefighters and walked the property edges, searching for the cause of the fire.

A black sedan rolled up, windows tinted, and Honey hugged her arms around her middle, wondering who it was. Lucas Hawk emerged from the vehicle in a dark suit, his gaze hooded as he scrutinized the scene.

Harrison strode around the side of the house, his gloved hand wrapped around the handle of a gas can. He met the fire chief and Lucas on the lawn near Lucas's car.

"I found this at the edge of the woods. Someone used it to set the blaze," Harrison said.

"The point of origin was the laundry room," the fire chief said. "I found signs of matches and smelled the gas there."

"Dammit, I hope he left prints on the can," Harrison said.

"Do you know who did this?" the fire chief asked.

Harrison shook his head. "Not yet. But I'll catch the son of a bitch. He didn't hurt anyone this time, but he could have."

"You think it was kids or vandals?" Lucas asked. "Or someone who owned one of these houses wanting to collect on insurance."

Harrison shifted. "No." He explained to Lucas about the threats against Honey.

"I'm sorry someone is trying to scare you off," Lucas said. "You don't deserve this."

Honey offered a small smile. "I'm just glad no one else was around or hurt."

The fire chief tilted his hat. "When things cool, we'll process the scene."

Harrison nodded and thanked him, and she followed him back to Lucas's sedan. "Did you talk to the Ritters?" Harrison asked.

Lucas pulled a photo from his car and handed it to Harrison. Honey's heart melted at the sight of the little red-haired girl with braids.

"Her name was Trish," he said. "She was eight years old and infatuated with cats. Parents took her to a town fall festival. There were games and a cakewalk and pony rides. The mom went to get popcorn and drinks while the little girl rode, but the lady manning the ponies said Trish ran off, chasing a kitty. They searched the festival and town, put up fliers, did everything they could think of, but never saw or heard from her again."

"She looks so innocent," Honey said, her emotions on her sleeve.

"This is beginning to sound like a pattern," Harrison said. "I can't believe no one saw it before."

"Information sharing and access to information across territories, especially in small towns, wasn't as easy back then as it is now," Lucas said.

Harrison heaved a disgusted breath. "I know. But somehow this creep got away with kidnapping children for nearly two decades and no one saw the pattern."

"Maybe because he traveled from one place to another," Lucas pointed out.

Honey's gut tightened. What if Chrissy and/or these other little girls had been kidnapped by someone who'd taken them out of the country?

She closed her eyes and said a silent prayer that they hadn't fallen prey to one of those soulless child-theft rings.

Or to a sexual predator or a captor who'd done unspeakable things to them.

HARRISON READ THE fear on Honey's face and wanted to comfort her. Lucas stepped away to answer the phone.

"I'm sorry about the house," he said to Honey.

"The house doesn't matter," Honey said. "Finding out what happened to these little girls and to Chrissy does."

How could he ever have wondered if Honey had lied to protect her father? She'd been almost as traumatized as he and his family by what had happened.

Lucas pocketed his phone as he approached. "Bad news. Dexter has been searching for other cases that might be connected to this one. Campers found a little girl's body in the mountains. It could be related."

Or it could be Chrissy. Harrison felt as if he'd been hit in the belly. "We should go."

Lucas nodded. "Get in. I'll drive."

Harrison glanced at Honey. "We can drop you off at my place."

Honey shook her head. "No, I'll go with you. There's no way I could sleep right now."

He climbed in the front seat and Honey in the back, and they settled in for the drive.

"Did they identify the girl?" he asked Lucas as Lucas veered onto the highway leading toward the mountains.

"Not yet," Lucas said, his voice on edge. "They think she's been there for a while, though."

Harrison swallowed bile.

Lucas's hands closed around the steering wheel in a white-knuckle grip as he drove. Farmland gave way to desertlike terrain, the thick boulders and rocks a testament they were getting close.

Harrison's mind raced with questions as they crossed the miles. If this body was Chrissy, whoever had taken her had a car...

"I checked on Williams," Lucas said. "He was nowhere near Austin or Corpus Christi when the other girls disappeared."

Damn, if the cases were connected, Williams wasn't their guy.

The sedan bounced over the ridges and rough terrain as Lucas sped toward the flashing lights. He wove around a curve and then they were there.

Dread clenched Harrison's stomach as they climbed from the car and met the detective.

He gestured toward an old mine. "Hikers ducked

in to seek shelter and found the body. No ID on her and she's pretty decomposed. But a pair of pink socks were half-buried in the dirt, still attached to the skeletal feet."

Harrison pinched the bridge of his nose as sorrow overcame him.

Lucas looked pale and leaned against a boulder for a moment, and Harrison felt Honey's hand go to his back. He breathed in and out deeply to stem the nausea.

This could be it. The day they'd finally found their sister.

But if it was her, there wouldn't be much left.

# Chapter Twenty

Honey's stomach rolled as she glanced toward the cave.

Whether the girl was Chrissy or another child, she hadn't deserved to be left dead—or to die—in a cave alone in the middle of nowhere. In a place where animals roamed freely at night, hunting for food.

A shiver rippled up her spine, and Honey caught Harrison's arm. "You don't have to go inside. Why don't you let the medical examiner handle it?"

Harrison stepped away from her. "This is my job, Honey. And that girl may be my sister. You can't possibly understand what that means."

Hurt swamped Honey at his tone, and she dropped her hand.

His gaze met hers, his pain so intense it pulsed through her own body.

The detective gestured toward the cave. "Let's go."

Lucas and Harrison followed the man up the incline where they met two other law enforcement officers. They handed Harrison and Lucas flashlights, and the men ducked inside the opening and disappeared into the darkness.

HARRISON STRUGGLED TO mentally remove himself from the possibility that the skeleton they were looking at might be Chrissy.

He wanted to remember her the way she was, with chubby cheeks, a gap-toothed smile and pigtails. With an infectious laugh and an annoying way of tagging after him and his brothers. With ice cream smeared on her face as she licked her cone.

The detective introduced them to the medical examiner, a middle-aged man named Dr. Thoreau. "Was there anything about your sister that would help identify her?"

Harrison and Lucas exchanged questioning looks.

"Had she broken any bones?" the doctor clarified. "Had any injuries?"

"She sprained an ankle once jumping from the swing at the playground," Harrison said. "But I don't recall her breaking any bones."

"Me, neither," Lucas said.

"Well, this girl did," the doctor said. "It looks like her femur was completely shattered."

"Did the killer do it?" Harrison asked.

The ME shrugged. "I don't think so. I think it happened when she was much younger. Judging from her bones, it looks like it healed but not properly."

Which meant this probably wasn't Chrissy. Although they still needed to wait on the autopsy.

"How long has the body been here?" Lucas asked.

The doctor shrugged. "Years. I'll call in a forensic specialist to help us narrow down the time frame and cause of death."

Lucas jammed his hands into the pockets of his

slacks. "Let me know what you find so we can compare to the FBI's database and NCMEC. We also have a forensic artist who does facial reconstruction."

"Have you searched the mine?" Harrison asked.

The detective rubbed his temple. "We did a preliminary search in case there were more bodies, but didn't find one. We'll process again for forensics."

"Lucas and I want to look around," Harrison said.

The detective nodded agreement, and Harrison and Lucas tugged on gloves, then used their flashlights to illuminate the interior as they examined the area where the body lay.

Harrison stooped to study a clump of dirt and found a book of matches that were half-rotted along with kindling as if someone had built a fire inside. Kids or hiker/campers, although they weren't very smart. There could be gas pockets inside and the place could have exploded.

The tunnel led to a section that had once been excavated, then parted in two directions. Lucas took one and Harrison inched into the other. The space was small, ceiling low, dark and dank, and somewhere ahead water trickled.

His foot hit something, and he shone the flashlight on it and realized he'd stepped on a beer can. Moving deeper, he scanned the floor and walls, then something shiny glinted in the darkness.

He inched toward it, then dropped to his knees and aimed his light on it. Something was almost buried in the dirt. He dug the dirt away with his fingers, his breathing puffing into the enclosed space as he struggled for air.

The dirt gave way to a silver chain. Frowning, he dug more dirt away until he freed the chain.

He held it up, studying it. It was an old-fashioned pocket watch. Not one a little girl would have, but a man.

Had it belonged to the girl's killer?

HONEY RUBBED HER arms to chase the chill away as she watched medics bring the body out and load it to transport to the morgue.

Harrison and Lucas finally emerged, both ashen faced and grim. She joined them with the detective by the ME's vehicle.

Harrison lifted a silver pocket watch and showed it to the detective. "I found this inside. It could belong to one of the miners or someone exploring the cave. But it's possible it was the killer's."

Lucas bagged it. "I'll get it to the FBI's lab right away."

Dr. Thoreau opened the driver's side of his vehicle. "I'll let you know as soon as I finish the autopsy and the forensic artist does her thing. I'll also send those samples to the lab as you requested and fax you the results."

The men shook hands and the ME climbed in his vehicle and took off.

Harrison and Lucas headed toward Lucas's sedan and she climbed in the back seat.

But the image of that pocket watch nagged at Honey as Lucas drove away.

Someone she'd known as a kid had a pocket watch.

Her father?

She racked her brain but couldn't remember him owning one.

Fatigue pulled at her, but every time she closed her eyes, she saw the girl's skeleton. Vacant pockets where her eyes had been. Bones brittle and decayed.

Lucas and Harrison had lapsed into a strained silence, the tension thick with unanswered questions.

"Do you think we should talk to Mother?" Lucas asked as he made the turn to Lower Tumbleweed.

"Not until we know something for certain," Harrison said.

Lucas agreed, then pulled up to the ruins of her father's house. The scent of burned wood, grass and leaves permeated the area, smoke clogging the air. A few embers still sparkled in the debris, but a fire worker remained to monitor the area in case the sparks reignited and started to spread.

They all climbed from the sedan and the Hawk men stepped near Harrison's SUV and conferred for a moment while Honey retrieved her keys and unlocked her van.

"What about Honey?" she heard Lucas murmur to Harrison. "Is she in a hotel?"

"She's going to stay at my place," Harrison said in a low voice.

A breeze stirred the smoke again, reminding her of the fact that someone burned down her house tonight.

"What's going on with you two?" Lucas asked.

Harrison muttered something beneath his breath. "Nothing. I'm the sheriff and she's in danger. I'm just doing my damn job."

Honey opened her van door and slid inside. Harrison was right. Nothing was happening between them.

It couldn't.

Even though she wanted him with every breath of her being.

HARRISON WAITED FOR Honey to park at his cabin before he went inside. He'd lied through his teeth to Lucas.

Well, maybe not lied...

There was nothing really between him and Honey, except...this tension. Sexual tension he had to resist.

Hell, after seeing her work in Austin, his admiration for her had risen even more.

Liking her and wanting her was messing with his mind.

"I need to shower," he said as they entered his cabin. He desperately had to wash the stench of the mine and what he'd seen off him. The acrid odor of smoke and sweat also permeated his skin.

"I need a shower, too," Honey said.

She slipped into the guest room, and he gritted his teeth as the shower water kicked on. Dammit, he wanted to strip and join her. Work off some of his nerves and anxiety and hunger for her by pounding himself inside her body.

He wanted to wipe the pain and fear off her face and make her smile and whisper his name in the throes of passion.

Anything to erase the memory of that skeleton from his mind.

He ducked into his room, removed his clothes and stepped into the shower. The hot water soothed the knots in his shoulders, and he soaped and scrubbed his skin and hair, washing away the odors of the night.

He wished he could wash away the ugliness in his soul, the pure bitterness and hate he had for the person who'd taken Chrissy and destroyed his family.

The water grew cold, and he stepped from the shower and dried off, then slipped on clean jeans and threw on a T-shirt. The cabin felt warm from the Texas heat, and outside the trees stood motionless with the lack of a breeze.

He ran a towel over his wet hair then shoved it back off his forehead with one hand and strode into the den. He went straight to the bar and poured himself a whiskey.

The guest bedroom door opened, and Honey appeared, wearing a tank top and pair of thin cotton pajama bottoms. His mouth watered as he looked her over.

Her long golden hair hung in damp strands around her shoulders, framing her beautiful face. Void of makeup, she looked impossibly young and innocent. Her rose-colored lips accentuated her pale skin and triggered wicked thoughts of kissing her again.

"I understand today was hard for you," she said in a low voice.

HE TOSSED THE drink down, then poured another. Honey walked toward him then picked up a second highball glass.

"Mind if I have one?"

He shook his head. "Sorry, I should have asked. I—"

"You don't have to explain," she said softly.

He averted her gaze and focused on pouring her whiskey to keep from touching her. But when he turned to hand the glass to her, and their fingers brushed, a current of need shot through him.

Her eyes widened as if she felt it, too. As if she shared that same need.

He hastily walked away, stood in front of the French doors leading to the back porch and stared at the view of Hawk's Landing that stretched behind his cabin. This ranch was beautiful, but he hadn't enjoyed it in years for dwelling on his family's sorrow.

Behind him, he heard Honey approach. Then he felt her stroke his shoulder, and he groaned.

"I'm sorry, Harrison. It's been a rough day."

He nodded. "For you, too."

"Like I told you, that house means nothing."

But it was her childhood home. It held bad memories of a life when she'd felt unwanted.

Yet she'd come so far since. In spite of the cold way his mother and the people in Tumbleweed had treated her, she'd grown into a loving, caring woman and made a success out of herself. Here, today, she'd been threatened and her house had burned down in front of her eyes, yet she seemed more concerned about him than herself.

He tossed the second drink down, then faced her. The compassion and yearning in her eyes shredded his last bits of composure.

He set the glass on the side table, then took a step closer to her. Her eyes darkened. Her lips parted on a breathy sigh.

He slipped her empty glass from her hand and set it beside his own. Then he yanked her into his arms and closed his mouth over hers.

HONEY DIDN'T KNOW what to think. She'd heard Harrison say there was nothing between them, yet all she *could* think at the moment was how much she wanted him and that he wanted her.

And after all they'd been through, there was no way she would deny him. Or herself.

Pleasure rarely came to her and she wanted it now. Wanted this time with him. Wanted to feel what it was like to be naked with Harrison, to be held in his arms and loved by him.

Even if it only lasted tonight.

He plunged his tongue inside her mouth and she met him thrust for thrust. Her arms slid around his neck, her body fitted hot and close against his as he drew her hips into the V of his thighs.

Hunger, need and desire exploded inside her, and she murmured his name, silently begging him not to stop. Not ever.

He cupped her hips with his hands and thrust his hard length against her belly and she moaned his name.

The clothes were too much.

They had to go.

She was emboldened by the passion in his touch as he raked kisses along her neck and jaw and trailed one hand over her breast. Gently he stroked her ripe nipple until it ached for his mouth, and she pushed his shirt off his shoulders.

He hadn't bothered to button it, thank God, or she would be ripping buttons in her haste.

With one quick flick of her hand, she dropped the garment to the floor and drank in his bare chest. Bronzed, wide shoulders led to taut muscles in his arms and chest that hardened and flexed beneath her gaze. She traced her fingers down his chest to the waistband of his jeans.

His breath hissed out. "Honey…"

"Yes," she breathed against his chest as she teased his nipple with her tongue.

He threw his head back and moaned, allowing her access, and she kissed and stroked his chest and abdomen, tasting the salty skin of his washboard abs and lower to his belt line where she yanked the snap on his jeans free and slid her hands inside to stroke his waist and hips.

He groaned again, then pushed her away, swung her up in his arms and carried her to his bedroom. He closed the door with his foot and laid her on his massive oak bed, then stopped and stared at her with hooded eyes.

She was afraid he'd change his mind, but instead he released a guttural groan, half pain, half pleasure. "Honey, I wish I didn't want you but I do."

Hurt wavered with the heat his words evoked. She started to get off the bed and run, to try to save herself from the memory of his touch so later she wouldn't be tormented by it, but he growled and shook his head, then leaned close to her and kissed her again.

This time a fever broke loose in her body, the throbbing need so intense, she forgot everything except that she had to have him.

She raked her nails down his bare back as he climbed on the bed on top of her, then she shoved at his jeans. He pushed at her pajama bottoms just as frantically, and she kicked them away, leaving her wearing a tiny white lace thong and tank top. He lowered his mouth and kissed her neck and throat, his fingers toying with her nipples through the thin fabric. His hot breath bathed her neck and breasts as he lifted her top over her head and tossed it to the floor. She heaved a breath and closed her eyes, savoring the sensations spiraling through her as he tugged one nipple between his teeth.

She clawed at him, wanting him closer. But he took his time, suckling one nipple then the next, triggering erotic sensations to stir in her womb and rise to a crescendo.

His lips found her belly button next, and he licked and teased his way along the lace line of her panties, then tugged them away and fused his mouth to her center.

She cried out as he lifted her hips, tossed the panties aside and took her sweet nub into his mouth.

Her body quivered in ecstasy and she groaned his name, losing herself in the moment as he brought her to the brink of release.

When he pulled away, leaving her aching, she whispered his name in a plea. He smiled through eyes glazed with passion, then snatched a condom from the bedside table, rolled it on and shoved her legs apart.

Wet, slick and needy, she opened for him, clinging to him as his sex teased her opening. He moved against her, stroking her inner thighs with his fingers until she practically begged him to join his body with hers.

And he did.

One quick hard thrust, and his thick manhood filled the emptiness inside her. She cried his name as sensations overcame her and her body exploded in a frenzy of mindless heat and pleasure. He stroked and rubbed her with his sex, pulling out and thrusting again, tormenting her with the force of his hunger.

Her body shook and quivered, and she wrapped her legs around him, pulling him deeper inside her until she felt him stiffen, then tense.

She sucked at his neck and raked her hands over his butt, thrusting her hips upward. He buried his head in her neck and moaned as he came apart inside her.

# Chapter Twenty-One

Harrison's body shook with the force of his release.

He breathed against Honey's neck, savoring the feel of her soft skin and body beneath his.

Unexpected emotions pummeled him, and he held her tighter, willing himself to maintain control. He'd had sex with plenty of women before, but he'd never made love.

Love?

He couldn't love Honey Granger.

She whispered his name against his chest, and he stilled and looked into her eyes. He feared he'd see regret and she'd shove him away, but instead passion glazed her expression and a soft smile lit her normally sad eyes.

God, she was beautiful when she smiled.

He wanted to erase the sadness forever.

Fear nearly choked him. How could he do that?

She rubbed his back, planted a kiss on his chest, then cupped his face between her hands and drew him closer for another long, heated, mind-blowing kiss.

He forgot all reason and kissed her again, loving the way their bodies fitted together and the way she clung to him.

He rolled her sideways, then slowly extricated himself, dropped a kiss into her hair, then slipped from bed and padded to the bathroom to dispose of the condom. A quick look in the mirror and he didn't recognize himself.

Hunger and raw desire darkened his eyes and made him look primitive and rough.

He washed up, then glanced at Honey through the crack in the door. She lay naked, tangled in the sheets, and she'd turned to her side, facing him. Her hair draped one sexy bare shoulder and spilled across the pillow, the pale moonlight streaming through the window creating a soft glow. She looked like a cross between an angel and a sex goddess.

Desperate need burned through him. He didn't stop to analyze it. There would be time for that when she left Tumbleweed.

Right now she was here, in his bed, naked and hot from his loving. He wanted to keep her there a little longer.

Heart hammering, he strode back to the bed. One knee hit the mattress, then the other. He tilted Honey's chin up with his thumb. Her lips parted, her breath puffed out. Her gorgeous breasts rose and fell, her nipples' stiff buds begging for his touch.

He complied. First with his hands, and then with his mouth.

She gave in return, kissing and suckling his neck, raking her fingers across his back, then his butt, then guiding his sex to her. He paused long enough to roll on another condom, then he parted her legs and stroked her sensitive nub.

She braced her hands on each side of him, rotating her hips in sensual decadence as she coaxed him deep inside her. He gripped her waist and thrust hard and fast, plunging in and out of her warm chamber, driving her to a frenzy of need that sent them both over the edge.

She cried out his name as her body quivered in release. Then she rotated her hips again, pumping his hard length until his body gave in to another orgasm. Sweet, blissful release overcame him, and he dragged her mouth to his, telling her with his moan and with his body how much she meant to him.

HONEY CLENCHED THE covers and willed this euphoria to last as Harrison disappeared into the bathroom again. She half expected to hear an apology, but instead he climbed back in bed, wrapped his arms around her and pulled her next to his hard body.

She smiled, pure bliss enveloping her, as she snuggled into him.

She'd been alone all her life. But tonight she'd made love to the man she'd fantasized about for years. It was even more wonderful than she'd imagined.

Harrison brushed her arm with his thumb, and she closed her eyes, content in his arms.

Fatigue dragged her into a deep sleep, and she dreamed that she and Harrison had made a life and a home together. They'd built a house on his ranch and they had horses and…a baby on the way.

She jerked awake, certain he'd be gone, but his arms were still wrapped around her and his breathing was shallow in sleep. She pressed her hand against his firm jaw. His beard stubble was rough, his lips parted, his face a picture of masculinity.

She planted a soft kiss on his cheek and closed her eyes again, treasuring the night as she fell asleep again.

Sometime later, a loud banging sound jarred her awake. Harrison bolted upright, then scrubbed his hand over his face as if he was disoriented.

The pounding continued. Someone was at the front door.

"Dammit." Harrison threw the covers aside, treating her to the sight of his hard, muscular body.

She silently groaned. She wanted to tell him to ignore the door and come back to bed. But the reality of the day before interceded, and she wrapped the sheet around her and ducked into the guest room while he yanked on clothes and hurried to the door.

In the guest room, she retrieved underwear, jeans and a T-shirt from her bag, and hurriedly dressed. It was probably Lucas with news from the lab, or maybe the fire chief...

She splashed cold water on her face, a tingle spreading through her at the sight of her red cheeks. Harrison's scruffy beard stubble had abraded her skin. Her hair was tousled, so she dragged a brush through it. Unable to tame the wild, wavy strands, she pulled it into a ponytail and secured it with a clasp.

Her body still smelled of Harrison, though. But if this was news about the case, they might need to act quickly.

Taking a deep breath, she walked into the den, which adjoined the kitchen. She veered toward it, hoping to brew a pot of coffee.

A loud gasp punctuated the air, and Honey froze.

"I heard there are other girls who disappeared like Chrissy, Harrison."

"Yes, Mother, I'm working on it—"

Honey bit her bottom lip, wishing she'd stayed in the bedroom.

Mrs. Hawk stalked into the room, arms folded, her eyes blazing with anger. She shot daggers at Harrison with her eyes. "My God, you're not working. You're shacking up with this whore instead."

ANGER AND HURT boomeranged inside Harrison. The pain of his mother's words on Honey's face shook him to the core.

"Mother," he said, not bothering to hide his disdain. "You have no right to speak to Honey like that. She has done nothing to hurt you or Chrissy and doesn't deserve the way you've treated her."

"She's that awful Granger man's daughter. And you know what his wife was—"

"Children are not a reflection of their parents, just as parents aren't a reflection of their children," Harrison snapped. He gave Honey an imploring look, hoping she understood the double meaning.

Honey folded her arms. "I'm sorry you feel that way, but more than that, I'm sorry for your loss," she said softly. "For the record, Harrison spent all day yesterday investigating Chrissy's case and the other girls' disappearances."

His mother started to speak but Honey cut her off.

"Also, someone burned my house down last night and your son was a complete gentleman. As the sheriff, he allowed me to stay in his guest room for my protection."

Harrison's pulse clamored. "You don't have to justify anything to my mother."

His mother spun toward him. "You're defending her over me."

"Do not go there, Mother," Harrison said. Because at this moment he would defend Honey. "And if you weren't so nasty to Honey, you'd realize that she is not to blame for Chrissy being gone. She left this town because of the ugly way you and others treated her. You should see the business she's built for herself. It's impressive, and she did it all on her own."

Honey arched a brow, seemingly surprised at his praise. But it was well earned.

His mother huffed. "All I want to know is if that body those detectives found was my little girl."

The raw agony in those words softened his anger. "How did you know about that?"

"I overheard Dexter and Brayden talking. You boys must be conspiring to leave me in the dark."

"Mother, stop it," he said, the chastising note back in his voice. "We will tell you something when we have answers. Actually this girl had suffered a broken femur at a young age, so we don't think it was Chrissy, but are waiting on confirmation."

He hadn't meant to sound harsh, but his mother staggered slightly as if she might faint.

Honey rushed forward to steady her. "Mrs. Hawk, why don't you sit down? I'll get you some coffee or tea—"

"I don't want anything to drink," his mother snapped. "I want my daughter back."

Honey nodded, sympathy in her eyes then started a pot of coffee.

Harrison pulled his mother into a hug. "I know, Mother. So do I."

But they both knew that was not likely. And he refused to promise his mother that he could make it happen.

His cell phone buzzed, and Harrison strode to the bedroom to retrieve it then answered. "Sheriff Hawk."

"It's Luke. Dammit, Harrison, another girl has disappeared."

Harrison's breath stalled in his chest. "Same age?"

"Yes. From Leadfoot Hollow about fifty miles from here. Nine-year-old girl named Kitty Walker. She and her big brother, George, were at a rodeo last night when the girl disappeared."

"Where are you?"

"On my way to get you."

"I'll be ready." He hung up and hurried to the den. He had to get his mother to leave. Honey could go with them.

He didn't intend to leave her in Tumbleweed alone. No telling what might happen to her while he was gone.

HONEY REMAINED SILENT as Harrison walked his mother to the door. "Mother, I promise, we'll call you when we know something."

His mother looked pale but nodded then gave Honey a sideways glance. Honey held her gaze. She refused to be intimidated.

Besides, it was obvious that Harrison's mother was suffering the deep-seated kind of pain only a mother who'd loved and lost her child could feel.

Not like Honey's own mother, who'd deserted her without ever looking back. She probably hadn't even shed a tear.

As soon as the door closed, Harrison snatched his keys. "We have to go. Another little girl is missing, not too far from here."

Honey gasped. "Oh, my God, what happened?"

"She and her big brother were at a rodeo last night."

Honey grabbed her purse while Harrison poured them both coffee in to-go mugs.

A minute later Lucas pulled into the drive and

honked. They raced to his sedan and Honey sipped her coffee as he peeled from the driveway.

"The local sheriff has had a search party looking for the girl all night," Lucas said. "Her mother does marketing for the rodeo. She knows a lot of the workers there and so do her kids, so she felt comfortable with the two of them hanging out until she finished last night."

"I assume they canvassed the workers and participants as well as attendees."

Lucas shrugged. "They did their best. Got all the employees for sure, but it was a late night and started raining so some of the ticket holders left early. Brother said he left the girl at the concession stand while he went to the bathroom. When he returned, he couldn't find her. That was close to eleven o'clock."

"Then he panicked, I guess," Harrison said.

"Not at first. He figured she went to the manager's office to see their mom, but she wasn't there. The mom paged the daughter, but she never showed." Lucas paused, voice troubled. "That's when they panicked. The staff checked the bathrooms, stalls, tents. It was a good hour before they called the sheriff."

He swung into a driveway for an older ranch home sitting on a hill in a neighborhood that had probably been built in the 1950s. A deputy sheriff's car was in the drive along with two other vehicles.

Lucas parked and the three of them walked up

the drive to the house. Harrison knocked, and an older woman with a gray ponytail answered the door. "I'm a neighbor, Birdie Samson," the woman said. "I came to stay with Melody and George last night. They're not doing too well."

She stepped aside, and a thin woman in jeans and a T-shirt with black hair, crying into a handkerchief, sat hunched on the couch. A teenage boy with black hair sat beside her, his head bowed, body shaking.

Lucas and Harrison followed Birdie inside and introduced themselves to the deputy. Honey hung back, her heart aching as she scanned the wall of photographs in the entry.

Photos of the boy and his sister riding horses. They looked young and happy and as if they were best friends.

She zeroed in on the little girl's face and her stomach twisted. She reminded her of Chrissy. Same age. Same innocent look.

Braided pigtails. Bright ribbons in her hair.

Just like Chrissy and the other victims.

# Chapter Twenty-Two

Harrison cleared his throat. "Mrs. Walker, tell us what happened last night."

She twisted her hands around the handkerchief. "We went to the rodeo like usual. The people there are like a family, so I let George and Kitty be on their own a little. I...guess I shouldn't have."

"It's understandable that you feel comfortable there," Harrison said. "I know the sheriff issued an Amber Alert and you gave him a photograph of Kitty. Is there anyone at the rodeo who paid a particular interest in Kitty?"

"She loves everyone," Mrs. Walker said. "The cowboys treat her like a kid sister, and the vendors like she's their daughter."

"I'm compiling a list of all the employees and rodeo riders and will run background checks," Lucas said. "Was there anyone new working last night?"

The woman fidgeted. "Not that I know of. Larry, the owner, usually vets everyone before he hires them."

"Can you give me his number, ma'am?" Lucas asked. "I want to get on that right away."

She grabbed a sticky note pad on the table and scribbled down a name and number, then handed it to Lucas. He excused himself and stepped into the other room to make the call.

George pinched the bridge of his nose, and Harrison's chest squeezed. "George, did you notice anyone paying attention to your sister?"

His brown eyes looked tortured as he looked up at Harrison. "Not really. She was talking to the clowns before they took to the ring. Then she wanted snacks, so she went to the concession stand while I went to take a leak."

"George," his mother admonished.

"It's fine, Mrs. Walker," Harrison said. "Let him tell things his way." He gave George a sympathetic look. "So you left her at the stand and when you got back, she wasn't there."

"No," George's voice cracked. "I was…mad at first. I figured she went back to the stands where we were sitting or to the stables to see the horses, but I checked both places and she wasn't there."

"Was she shy around strangers?" Harrison asked.

"No. She talked to everybody," George said. "A couple of times she wandered off and joined a bunch of kids who'd come for a birthday party. She wanted some cake and ice cream." He wiped at his eyes. "She loved balloons and was always sneaking over to play with them during the show."

"She liked the souvenir stands, too," Mrs. Walker said. "She collected the little stuffed ponies."

"You checked those stands?" Harrison asked.

"Yeah," George said. "She stopped at Benny's

booth and talked to some other kids. Benny said this big guy, older, about your age, was right in the middle of them." He blushed as if he hadn't meant to imply that Harrison was old.

"A big guy? You mean a father?" Harrison asked.

"No," George said. "This guy was mentally challenged. He talked like a kid."

Harrison swallowed. Something about the story rang a bell.

A PICTURE OF what had happened flashed in Honey's mind.

"Tell me more about the man," Honey said.

George bounced his knee up and down. "He didn't talk very plain, sort of made a weird noise. He was intrigued with the colored streamers at the booth. He touched one of my sister's ribbons and told her how pretty it was."

A sense of déjà vu swept over Honey, stirring a memory of Chrissy twirling her hair ribbons around her finger one day at the park in town. Then Elden ran up and talked to Chrissy. He wanted to touch Chrissy's ribbons.

Honey had felt sorry for Elden because the other kids made fun of him. He had no friends, so she'd encouraged Chrissy to be nice to him. That day he'd followed them all over the park...

"What was this guy's name?" she asked, her throat thick with fear.

George shrugged. "I don't know. But some lady

stormed up and took his hand and told him to come with her. She sounded mad."

Elden's mother?

Honey's stomach clenched.

Oh, God...

She covered her mouth to stifle a gasp and stood.

Harrison's hand brushed over hers. "What is it, Honey?"

She glanced at George, then at his parents, and suddenly felt sick. "I need some air."

Harrison's brows arched, but he nodded, and she raced from the room. Seconds later he joined her outside. She was leaning against his SUV, perspiration beading her forehead and neck as she fought nausea.

Harrison's boots crunched the gravel as he approached. "Honey, what's wrong?"

She inhaled a deep breath. "The mentally challenged guy the little girl was talking to... I think it was Elden."

He took her arm and forced her to face him. "Elden?"

She pushed her hair behind one ear. "In Yvonne's diary, she mentioned a boy teasing her. Something about that pocket watch seemed familiar, and I remember now that Elden had one. He tied a ribbon to it and was mesmerized by it as he swung it back and forth."

Harrison's eyes widened as he considered her theory. "But we found the ribbon at your dad's house."

"He or his mother could have put it there," Honey said. "At the park one day, Elden was intrigued with Chrissy's ribbons and… Oh, God, it's all my fault."

Harrison's jaw tightened. "What do you mean?"

"I told Chrissy he was harmless, to be nice to him, and she let him touch her hair ribbons." She'd thought Elden was harmless, but what if she was wrong?

The color drained from Harrison's face. "I wonder if he was at the bluff that night."

Honey strained to recall the faces she'd seen, but she'd been so disappointed that Harrison was meeting another girl that she hadn't stayed long. "I don't know." She wiped at her forehead. "Although if the same person hurt all these girls, that means he was in different places. Elden doesn't drive—"

"His mother could have taken him to the rodeo and the carnival. Those are all places kids like to go," Harrison said between gritted teeth.

Horror engulfed Honey. If that was true, and Elden was guilty, his mother had known and covered for him.

Lucas strode toward them. "Larry wasn't any help. No new employees that stuck out as suspicious. What's going on?"

Harrison quickly explained Honey's theory.

Lucas jangled his keys. "I'll drop you at your car and do some checking on Elden and his mother while you drive out to the Lynches' house."

They quickly climbed in Lucas's car and Harrison phoned a local judge for a warrant. If Honey was right, Elden might have Kitty now.

She closed her eyes and prayed they found the little girl in time.

HARRISON'S STOMACH CHURNED as Lucas dropped him and Honey at his SUV. He had phoned his deputy to fill him in on the drive, and Mitchell was supposed to be canvassing the town in case Elden and his mother were at the diner or shopping.

He flipped on the siren and pressed the accelerator. Honey fidgeted nervously. "I never thought he was dangerous."

"Me, neither," Harrison admitted. "And his mother always kept him on a short leash."

"What if that's the reason she did?" Honey asked. "Maybe he was different when he was alone. Maybe he had a bad temper and snapped?"

Harrison raked a hand through his hair, weaving around traffic. Sadly, he'd never thought Elden completely understood what was going on. But maybe he had. Still, why hurt little girls?

He stopped at the judge's house to pick up the warrant, then hurried back to the car and raced away. He rounded a curve, tires squealing, and bounced over a rut in the road as he flew toward Lower Tumbleweed. Elden and his mother lived in a mobile home not far from the Grangers' house.

He turned into the drive for the mobile home

park, slowing in case children were outside. A swing set and jungle gym had been added to a central area, creating a park for the kids. He scanned it to see if anyone was there. If Elden was a child predator, he had the perfect hunting ground.

Although none of the victims had lived in his neighborhood.

He screeched to a stop in the drive, then jumped out. Honey started behind him, but he gestured for her to wait. If Elden was guilty and his mother was protecting him, she might be dangerous.

He strode up the three steps to the door and knocked. "Mrs. Lynch, open up, please, it's Sheriff Hawk."

Nothing.

He banged harder and shouted again, but no one answered, so he jiggled the doorknob. It was locked. Dammit.

He had a warrant but that didn't give him a right to break in. But a little girl's life was in danger...

He jammed his lock-picking tool into the lock, then twisted it until the door popped open.

The car door slammed behind him, and Honey got out. He motioned that it was okay for her to join him, and she ran up the steps. He pushed the door open and inched inside. "Anyone home?"

No answer.

Only the sound of a fan whirring.

He scanned the small living area with a frown. Elden's mother cleaned at the local inn and for others in the town. Her own place was sparsely furnished, the furniture old, but the room looked tidy and the kitchen was clean.

One corner of the den held a bookcase full of toys—building blocks, crayons and paper, toy cars and plastic animals—a sign of Elden's mental age.

"Look for anything that might belong to a little girl," he murmured.

Honey searched the bookcase while he walked down the narrow hall and glanced in the first bedroom. Elden's.

Blue-painted walls, a comforter with a farm animal theme, and posters of various rodeos and rodeo stars. He checked the desk and found art paper and crayons, then several drawings of little girls.

His gut tightened.

In each drawing, he'd sketched colored ribbons in the little girl's hair.

Anger and sorrow engulfed him.

He opened the closet door and dug through the man's clothes and shoes, his pulse jumping when he found a toy chest inside.

He lifted the lid and his heart stopped. All toys little girls would play with.

And other items—a pink backpack, a purple hair ribbon, a child's pink purse...

Had the items belonged to the missing girls?

Then a little beaded bracelet. Tears flooded his eyes. It was Chrissy's.

HONEY FOUND NOTHING in the kitchen or den and rushed to help Harrison in the bedroom. "Did you find anything?"

He was standing at the closet with his back to her, but he was so still she knew something was wrong. Then he slowly turned and she saw a child's bracelet in his hand.

"It was Chrissy's," he said in a tortured voice. "There are other things in there, too, from other girls."

Her breath caught at the implication. "Oh, Harrison. I'm sorry…"

His phone buzzed, and he whipped his head around as if physically jerking himself back to reality. "Sheriff Hawk." A pause. "No, they're not at the house, Lucas. But I found some things that belong to the little girls. Elden is our guy." Another pause. "Okay, let me know if you find something."

He hung up and wiped a hand over his eyes. "He's going to put a trace on the Lynches' phones."

Honey's skin prickled as she studied the drawings on Elden's desk. The little girls, the ribbons… then a sketch of the bluff and the swimming hole and the caves…then a second entrance, one she'd never been in.

Inside the cave, though, was a clump of rocks. A flower was sticking up between them.

Her heart hammered. "Harrison, look at this. This could be the place where he left the girls."

Harrison snatched the picture then took her hand. "Come on, we need to hurry. If he has Kitty, maybe we can save her."

# Chapter Twenty-Three

Harrison's pulse raced as he drove toward the bluff. He called Lucas and left him a message about the sketch.

Honey sat stone still in the seat beside him, except for her hands, which she kept twisting in her lap.

"I should have remembered about Elden and the pocket watch and his fascination with the ribbons earlier," Honey said in a strained voice.

"That would have been helpful."

Pain flashed in her eyes, and he regretted the bite to his voice, but he couldn't retract the words.

Neither could he forgive himself for not staying home and watching Chrissy that night. If he had, she'd be alive.

Although traffic was minimal, the minutes dragged as he drove over the terrain. Dark clouds hovered above the sky. They rarely got rain this time of year, but today's clouds looked dismal and threatening.

Honey stared out the window, her face ashen. He swung up the dirt road to the bluff, bypassing the scenic overhang, and barreled into the clearing where the teens usually parked.

A rusty black pickup sat sideways in front of a cluster of rocks. Elden's mother's truck.

"They're here."

Honey gripped the door handle as she scanned the area. "Look, Harrison, over there!"

He jerked his head to the left near the mouth of the cave and his blood ran cold. Elden was hunched low on the ground, his mother pacing beside him.

"Wait here!" he told Honey as he eased open his car door.

She shook her head and slid from the SUV. He motioned for her to stay by the car then laid his hand over his gun and stepped forward. Rocks crunched beneath his boots as he slowly walked toward them.

A low, wailing sound echoed from Elden, teeth jarring in its shrill intensity.

A coldness washed over Harrison. Elden was holding the little girl, Kitty, in his arms, rocking her back and forth, his body shaking with sobs.

Elden's mother swung around, eyes wild with terror and desperation. She aimed a gun at them.

Harrison halted, and Honey froze beside him.

"Stop, Sheriff," she growled. "Don't come any closer."

Harrison held up a warning hand. "Please, Mrs. Lynch. You don't want to shoot me or anyone else. This has to stop."

Her hand trembled as she waved the gun around. Somewhere in the distance a wild dog howled. Or maybe it was a coyote. "I have to protect my baby. That's what mamas do."

"That's true," Harrison said, his voice low, controlled. "But they don't murder for them."

"I haven't murdered anyone," she shouted.

"But Elden has, and if you're covering for him and letting him continue, then you are as much to blame as he is."

"He didn't mean to hurt them!" she cried. "He wanted to play with them."

Honey eased up beside him. "He likes the ribbons in their hair, doesn't he?" Honey said softly.

Mrs. Lynch's face crumbled. "He wanted to make friends. Kids laughed and teased him all his life, but he just wanted to play like they did."

"Only he was bigger and got rough," Harrison guessed.

Sorrow streaked her face as she glanced down at her son, who was wailing like an injured animal. "He tried to tell them how pretty they were, but they got scared and ran from him."

Harrison envisioned the scene she described, and felt like his heart had been shredded with a sharp knife. "Is that what happened with my sister?"

Tears leaked from the older woman's eyes and she nodded miserably. "I'm sorry. He didn't mean to hurt her. But she ran and he chased her like it was a game."

"It wasn't a damn game," Harrison bit out.

"No, but he thought it was. When he caught her, he tried to hug her, but…he hugged her too hard."

The breath whooshed from his lungs in an excruciating rush. "He smothered her?"

Misery emanated from the woman as she laid

a hand on her son's back. The gun bobbed in her trembling hand.

"It was an accident."

"Then you should have done the right thing and reported it." Harrison forced his voice to remain calm as he inched closer to the woman.

"But the state would have taken him away from me," she said on a sob. "Then he would have been stuck in some home and treated like an animal or a criminal. Poor Elden didn't deserve that."

"My sister didn't deserve to have her life snuffed out when she was ten," Harrison said bitterly. "Neither did the other little girls. And their families didn't deserve to lose their children."

"I know, and Elden and I are both sorry," Mrs. Lynch mumbled.

Harrison spoke through clenched teeth. "He was dangerous and should have been locked away so he couldn't hurt anyone else."

Honey eased toward Elden and spoke softly. "It's okay, Elden, do you remember me? I'm Honey."

"Stay back!" Elden's mother warned.

But Honey crept closer. "I just want to comfort him. Elden and I were friends. Weren't we, Elden?"

Mrs. Lynch looked rattled by Honey's tone, and Harrison took advantage of her distraction and jumped her. She screamed and swung the gun toward him, but he knocked her arm upward and the gunshot blasted the air.

She lost the grip on the weapon and it sailed through the air toward the cave and landed in the dirt.

"Mama!" Elden cried.

The woman pummeled Harrison with her fists, but he overpowered her, grabbed her arms and yanked them behind her.

"I just wanted to protect him!" she screamed as tears rained down her cheeks.

"What about those little girls?" Harrison growled next to her ear. "What about protecting them from your son?"

"He didn't mean to hurt them!" she cried again.

"But he did hurt them," Harrison said as he snapped handcuffs around her wrists. "And you stood by and let him."

HONEY'S HEART ACHED as she knelt beside Elden. He was hysterical, sobbing, rocking back and forth, his head buried against the little girl.

"It's me, Honey," she said softly. "I know you wanted to play with her, Elden." In spite of her terror for Kitty, she rubbed his back to calm him. "But you can let her go now. She needs to rest."

Tears blurred her eyes as she imagined him holding Chrissy this way, of his shock and frustration when she realized he'd hurt her.

He made a low, mewling sound, and she gently rubbed his arms. "Just lay her down gently," she said in a low murmur.

She continued to whisper soft words of encouragement until he eased the child to the ground. He spread her hair around her face and kissed her cheek, sobs racking his body.

Honey pressed her hand to the little girl's chest and suddenly realized she was still breathing. "Harrison, she's alive. Call 911!"

Elden sank back on the ground, wrapped his arms around himself and continued crying and rocking. Harrison quickly phoned an ambulance.

Honey cradled the little girl in her lap and gently smoothed the hair from her cheek. Seconds later Harrison joined her and checked the child's pulse. Relief filled his face when he realized she might make it.

Elden's mother rushed to her son, her arms still cuffed behind her back, and sank down beside him.

Harrison ordered her to stay beside him. "Where is my sister?"

"In the cave near that back entrance," the woman murmured. "Behind the rocks. I...put her there so she could rest."

Honey's chest heaved at the anguish in Harrison's expression. "And the other little girls?"

"They're all together," Elden's mother choked out. "I didn't want them to be alone."

"Except we found a child in the mountains."

"I didn't want to leave her, but I didn't have time to bring her back here."

"What about Honey's father?" Harrison bellowed. "Did you kill him?"

Her body shook with her sobs. "He started coming up here drinking and snooping around," she shouted. "I saw him in the cave. He found that damn ribbon."

Honey swallowed hard. "So you were afraid he'd find Chrissy and you killed him?"

"I couldn't let anyone take my baby away from me," she cried again. "He's just a kid…"

"You put the ribbon in my father's house to frame him," Honey said through clenched teeth.

Elden's mother nodded miserably again. "Your daddy was worthless. I figured the Hawks would believe it."

"And they did," Honey said. "But you could have saved these other children if you'd gotten Elden help."

"Did you threaten Honey and burn down the Grangers' house?" Harrison asked.

"I couldn't let her find the truth," Elden's mother cried. "Those houses needed to be torn down anyway."

"Let me call my brothers." Harrison stepped to the side and made a phone call. Honey heard him tell Lucas where they were and what had happened. "Bring shovels," he said. "We have to dig those rocks away to get to Chrissy."

A siren wailed, the shrill sound drowning out the

woman and her son's cries. Honey understood the need to protect a child, but not at the cost of other children's lives.

Nothing justified that.

EMOTIONS PUMMELED HARRISON as the paramedics and his brothers arrived. Time seemed to stand still as they waited to see if the little girl was all right. The medics gave her oxygen and she immediately stirred. She looked frightened and confused, but she was going to be fine.

He called the parents and told them to meet her at the hospital.

He forced Elden and his mother into the back of his SUV, both cuffed and restrained so they couldn't escape. Honey wanted to help, but he insisted it was dangerous and ordered her to remain outside while he and his brothers hurried into the cave with shovels and flashlights.

It took him no time to find the rocks as he'd noticed them earlier but had thought they'd fallen in a mining landslide. They eased away the rocks, stacking them to the side, and Harrison crawled through the opening.

A wave of sorrow and pain engulfed him when he saw the skeletal remains of his sister and three other girls lying side by side. Elden's mother had covered each of them with a blanket. Chrissy's rag doll was tucked beside her.

A strangled sound caught in his throat. His brothers' faces were etched in grief and horror.

Finding Chrissy and learning the truth about what happened to her should have given him peace.

But anguish filled him. And now they had to break the news to their mother.

## Chapter Twenty-Four

An hour later guilt still weighed on Honey as she watched Harrison and his brothers exit the cave with the ME. They had called in a team to remove the bodies and transport them to the morgue.

The identity of the girls had to be verified, families called, then the process of funeral arrangements made.

Harrison's mother was going to be devastated. But at least now she could give her daughter a proper burial and Chrissy could rest in peace.

And now Honey knew who'd killed her father, she could return to Austin and leave Tumbleweed behind.

Sun slanted off Harrison's strong jaw as he glanced up at her. The pain emanating from him made her want to go to him and soothe his anguish. But only time could do that.

The fact that she'd encouraged Chrissy to be nice to Elden meant she'd put Harrison's sister in danger. Granted, she'd been trying to do the right thing, but in doing so, she was responsible for Chrissy's death.

How could Harrison ever forgive her?

How could she forgive herself?

HARRISON COULD BARELY look at Honey. His family had blamed her and her father for his little sister's disappearance when all along they weren't responsible.

Elden was.

No one had ever thought to suspect him.

Honey had been nice to Elden, which might have contributed to the problem, but she'd been bullied and teased herself, and she'd simply been trying to be nice to a mentally challenged child.

How could he fault her for being a kindhearted, good person?

His deputy arrived, and Harrison turned Elden and his mother over to him. Mitchell would take care of locking them up and booking them.

The transport team drove away with the girls' remains, and grief and dread welled in his chest.

"We should talk to Mother," Dexter said.

Harrison nodded. They'd wait to notify the other families until they'd verified the girls' identities.

"I'll drop Honey off and meet you at the ranch."

His brothers agreed and they separated to go to their individual vehicles. Honey was waiting by the SUV, her sympathetic look mixed with other emotions he couldn't define.

"We're going to go see my mother and break the news," he said, his voice dark. "I'll drop you at my place. That is, unless you're ready to go back to Austin."

Honey's phone buzzed and she gave it a quick glance, but didn't answer. Instead she climbed in the passenger side in silence.

"I'm sorry, Harrison. If I hadn't encouraged Chrissy to be friends with Elden, she'd be alive."

The guilt in her voice triggered his own. It wasn't her fault. He should have been watching his sister that night.

But he was too emotional to speak. All he could think of now was the expression on his mother's face when he and his brothers delivered the news they'd found Chrissy and that she'd been dead all these years. That her body had been left to rot in a cold cave.

Honey turned to look out the window, and he sped toward his cabin, his body tight with anxiety.

He parked and turned to her, his heart hammering. "Now you know what happened to your father, what are you going to do?"

"I guess I'll get Dad's property cleaned up and put it on the market," Honey said.

"Then you're going back to Austin?"

"That's where my life is," she said quietly.

That was true.

The thought of her leaving made his throat thicken. But she had reason to hate Tumbleweed and as she said, she had a life in Austin. That guy she worked with was probably waiting on her.

She climbed out, and he started to ask her to stay, but that wouldn't be fair.

He had a rough time ahead at his mother's, too, and he needed to get going. Anything that had happened between him and Honey was due to the stress of the past few days.

She had given him no indication that she cared

about him or wanted to stay. That she might even love him.

So he gritted his teeth and let her climb from the SUV and head inside his cabin. With a heavy heart, he drove toward the farmhouse on Hawk's Landing to meet his brothers.

As HONEY WALKED through Harrison's cabin, the memory of making love to him made her heart ache with love. She wanted to stay, to comfort him when he returned, to tell him how much she cared for him.

But she didn't belong here. Not with a Hawk.

She had to tie things up and go back to Austin where no one knew the girl she'd been and the family she'd come from.

Where they only knew her as Honey Granger, the fixer-upper, the renovator/designer who turned crumbling properties into beautiful homes for families.

She repacked her suitcase, then drove to her old neighborhood. The devastation was stark, the scent of smoke and burned rubble so strong she had to inhale deep breaths to calm the queasiness in her stomach.

Queasiness from the destruction but also from the fact that the people who'd lived here had suffered, lost their homes to the bank and, now, to fire. And that other kids like her would grow up homeless, in shelters or on the streets because they had no good place to go.

Kids who'd be bullied and teased like she was.

Elden's face flashed in her mind, and as much as she regretted what he'd done, she couldn't have been mean to him years ago.

That would have been wrong, too.

Sympathy for him also filled her. He hadn't meant to hurt the girls. He'd simply wanted love and hadn't realized his own strength.

She hugged her arms around herself and turned in a wide arc to study the property. The neighborhood could hold at least ten to fifteen homes. Although three had completely burned down due to Elden's mother, ten others still stood in poor condition. Abandoned and left for dead.

A vision of what the houses could look like hit her, and adrenaline surged through her just as it did at the beginning of any new project.

She hadn't always believed in fate, but perhaps everything that had happened in her past and this past week was for a reason. She couldn't change anything in that past, but she could do something about the future.

She could give other children the kind of hope that she'd craved. And if she found some investors and financial assistance, she could give them an affordable home and prove to the people in Tumbleweed that she'd made something of her life.

Decision made, she retrieved her cell phone and called Jared to tell him her plans. Together they could put together a deal and make this burned-down, run-down neighborhood into something to be proud of.

HARRISON AND HIS brothers gathered around their mother in the den and delivered the news. Her face crumpled, but she seemed to accept the fact that Chrissy was gone as if in her heart she'd known it all along.

She knotted a tissue in her hands. "So Waylon Granger and his daughter had nothing to do with it?"

Harrison shook his head. "No, Mother. Elden was infatuated with little girls and drawn to the pretty ribbons in their hair. He's mentally challenged and didn't realize how big or strong he is and tried to hold them when they ran from him."

"He smothered them," Lucas said quietly.

A choked sob came from their mother. "Our poor little Chrissy lying up there all alone all these years."

Harrison's stomach twisted. The thought of Chrissy lying in that cold cave made him feel ill inside, as well. They had searched it so many times but never moved those damn rocks aside.

Brayden squeezed their mother's hand. "Elden's mother said she put the other girls there so they wouldn't be alone."

His mother gave him a sharp look as if that comment didn't offer any comfort. "What's going to happen to the Lynches?"

Harrison glanced at Dexter. Technically Elden was a serial killer although the circumstances were a consideration. "Elden will be charged, but considering his mental impairment, he'll go into a special facility where he'll be monitored. But he won't be able to go free and hurt anyone else."

"And his mother?"

"She'll be charged as an accomplice for covering up the crimes," Harrison said.

"The judge may be sympathetic to her," Dexter said. "But if she'd come forward and institutionalized Elden after he killed Chrissy, those other little girls would still be alive."

Harrison nodded. "I'm sorry, Mother. No one suspected Elden or noticed signs that he was violent. It really was more accident than intention. He... loved the girls."

Tears streamed down his mother's face. "It doesn't bring our little girl back, though."

"No," Harrison said softly. "But at least we know that she wasn't killed by a deviant who tortured her or inflicted unnecessary pain on her."

"We can give her a nice burial," Brayden added. "And now we'll have a place to visit her."

Their mother nodded and wiped at her tears. Dexter moved to the kitchen to make some tea while his mother retrieved the photo album she'd kept of Chrissy's childhood. They spent the next two hours looking at pictures and sharing memories of Chrissy.

She had been lost long ago, but at least they had her back now, and they would always remember her in their hearts.

THREE HOURS LATER Harrison left the ranch house. His mother had already started making arrangements for a service for Chrissy and was going to try to get some rest. Brayden offered to stay at the house with her that night while he and Dexter and Lucas left.

As they'd reminisced over Chrissy, he couldn't help but think about Honey. She had the answers she needed about her father. What was she going to do now?

His lungs squeezed for air as he remembered making love to her. And he had made love to her— it hadn't simply been sex.

He cared about Honey.

A pain ripped through him. His family had found closure, finally. But sometime during the last few days while he was looking for Chrissy and trying to find Waylon Granger's murderer, he'd fallen in love with Honey.

He pulled up to his cabin and instantly noticed that Honey's car was missing. Disappointment bombarded him. She couldn't have gone back to her father's. There wasn't enough house left to stay in.

He ran a hand through his hair as he parked and

walked up to the door. The house was dark when he entered, a lone lamp illuminating the den.

The floors creaked as he walked into the entry-way, the emptiness accentuating the loneliness engulfing him.

She was gone.

Dammit.

He flipped on a light and strode into the kitchen, then spotted a note lying on the table. Hope budded inside him.

Maybe she'd gone to the inn for the night and he would see her in the morning.

But emotions pummeled as he read the note.

Dear Harrison,
My heart aches for you and your family. I'm so sorry about Chrissy. I wish I could go back and change things, but I can't.

I can leave town, though, so your family can honor your sister the way Chrissy deserves without having me as a reminder of the past.

Take care of yourself, Harrison.
Goodbye,
Honey

Harrison crushed the note in his hands. He didn't want Honey to leave, but he couldn't blame her for hating this town after the way they'd treated her.

But dammit, he'd lost Chrissy a long time ago.

And now he'd just found Honey, and he'd lost her, too.

# Chapter Twenty-Five

The next week was hell.

Harrison tried to focus on his family's needs and his mother during the memorial service and his sister's burial, but all he could think about was Honey and why she hadn't stayed around to say goodbye to him in person. He'd called her numerous times, but she hadn't returned his call.

She obviously didn't love him.

She'd walked away without looking back, just as she'd left Tumbleweed years ago and lost touch.

Except she'd built a life for herself and a good reputation and business. And just this afternoon Geoffrey Williams had told him that she'd bought the land/lots in her father's neighborhood and planned to transform the area into affordable, nice homes for low-income families. How she planned to pull it off, he didn't know. But he trusted that Honey would do what she'd said.

She had integrity.

"She's back," Cora said as Harrison sipped his coffee.

"What?" For a moment, he was disoriented. "Who's back?"

"Honey Granger," Cora said. "They've already started bulldozing that land where her daddy lived.

Leroy Pirkle and Betty Sumner saw the plans for the development and it's quite impressive."

Leroy and Betty were on the town council.

"Honey is here herself or did she send her co-worker?" He'd heard that her partner, Jared, had met with Leroy and Betty.

"I saw her van myself," Cora said. "Not sure how long she's staying, but she booked a room at the inn for two weeks."

Harrison's pulse jumped, but he forced himself to remain passive. He hadn't yet told anyone, including his family, how he felt about Honey.

But he missed her like crazy. And he wanted her back in his life.

*She left you without saying goodbye.*

That had hurt.

Except he'd reread her note a hundred times and sensed she thought she didn't belong in this town.

She was wrong.

He stood and tossed some cash on the table to pay for his lunch. "Thanks. I gotta go."

Cora smiled, took the money along with his empty coffee cup and dish and sauntered toward the kitchen.

Heat suffused him, nearly robbing his breath, as he stepped outside. Three buildings down, his gaze zeroed in on the jewelry store.

He had no idea how Honey felt about him, but he knew how he felt about her. And it was damn time he told her.

She might laugh in his face or tell him to get lost, but this time if Honey Granger left Tumbleweed, she'd know that she was loved and that at least one person wanted her to stay forever.

ADRENALINE SURGED THROUGH Honey as she watched the bulldozer clear the burned rubble from her father's house and the neighboring properties. She had worked with Jared and an architect to design a street lined with Craftsman and ranch homes that would provide comfortable, affordable homes and add value to the town of Tumbleweed.

She'd spent the last week working on the plans, drawing designs and soliciting financial assistance. She was also using local building companies, suppliers and workers, which would feed money back into the community.

She couldn't wait to see the houses popping up and families moving in.

"This is going to be fabulous," Jared said. "But you know this project will take time."

Honey nodded. She wanted to be here every step of the process, but that would mean she'd be close to Harrison.

Too close.

She couldn't stay here and not want him.

"Are you interested in overseeing it?" Honey asked.

Jared's eyes widened in surprise. "I thought you'd do that. I know this was your hometown."

"It was, but I have mixed memories here and—"

Harrison's SUV rolled down the street, cutting off the rest of her statement. Her breathing turned choppy, a blend of nervous anticipation and sadness.

The owner of the bulldozer shouted that he needed to talk to them, and she gestured for Jared to handle him.

Harrison parked on the side of the street, his big body taut with tension as he strode toward her.

She told herself to run. To get in her car and drive away before she did something stupid like admit that she was in love with him.

"I heard what you're doing," he said in a gruff voice.

She nodded. "It's a good business move." Although business really had nothing to do with it. Her heart was in this project because like it or not, part of her heart was still here.

With Harrison.

His dark gaze met hers as if he recognized the lie. She averted her gaze, determined to keep her emotions at bay, but she could smell his masculine scent and the aftershave that had lingered on her skin after they'd made love, and tears burned the backs of her eyelids.

He took her hand and pulled her beneath a sawtooth tree away from the work crew and Jared.

"Honey," he said on a deep breath. "I had to see you."

"What's wrong?" she said. "Did Elden or his mother get out?"

"No, they're both locked away now, and all the families have been notified." He scrubbed a hand over his face. "The people, little girls, in town are safe."

She breathed out in relief. "Good. I know it hasn't been easy on your family and your mother."

He released a weary breath. "No, but she's holding up. But that's not what I wanted to talk to you about."

Heat seared her skin where he was still holding her hand. She should let go. Put some distance between them. But she couldn't bring herself to break the moment.

He lifted her hand and kissed her palm and her heart melted. "I'm glad you came back," he said in a low voice. "I...missed you."

"Harrison, don't—"

"Why not?" His voice grew stronger, and he cupped her face between his hands. "When you left, I realized how much I missed you, how much you meant to me." His eyes darkened, and he slid one hand into his pocket.

Her breath caught as he opened his palm to reveal a stunning diamond in an antique setting. "I love you, Honey. I want you to marry me."

Oh, God, she wanted that, too. She loved him with all her heart. She probably always had.

She always would.

But his mother hated her.

And there was no way she could come between them.

"I'm sorry, Harrison, it would never work."

Pain flashed in his eyes. "Because you don't feel the same way."

"Because I'm Honey Granger, the girl your mother has always despised. She thinks I'm a tramp and that I'm not good enough for you."

"I don't give a damn about what she thinks," he said. "Besides, she's wrong."

"Well, I care what she thinks," Honey said. "She's your mother and you love her. Your family has been through enough. I certainly won't be the reason for more tension and unhappiness between you."

"But Honey—"

She pressed her finger to his lips. "No, Harrison." She closed his fingers around the ring and kissed his cheek. "Thank you, but no, I can't marry you. I'm leaving my partner in charge of the project and I'm leaving town tonight."

She hadn't planned that, but now that he'd proposed she had to. If she stayed another minute, she'd back down, confess her love and throw herself at him.

Her chest burned with the pressure of holding back her tears, and she rushed to her van, climbed inside and sped away from the curb. She glanced in the rearview mirror and wished she hadn't. He stood ramrod still, his handsome face etched in hurt, staring after her.

But she didn't turn back. She told herself to keep driving until she reached Austin.

HARRISON MET HIS brothers at the Broken Spoke for a beer to drown his sorrows.

"You look like someone shot you," Lucas said.

Dexter elbowed him as he poured himself a beer from the pitcher. "Or run over you."

Brayden took a mug for himself. "Yeah, what gives?"

Honey had turned him down, that was what was wrong.

She must not love him.

"If you're worried about Mom, I think she's okay," Brayden said.

"Yeah, except she hates Honey," Harrison muttered in frustration.

"What does that matter?" Dexter asked.

Harrison stared into his beer, sullen and brooding.

"Uh-oh," Lucas said. "I know what's wrong. You fell for Honey, didn't you?"

Harrison cut his eyes toward Lucas. "She's nothing like what Mom thought."

"I know," Brayden said. "Hell, have you seen the houses she's renovated in Austin? They're amazing."

"And she's doing that here in Lower Tumbleweed," Dexter said, a hint of awe in his voice.

Misery clawed at Harrison. "She's pretty amazing."

Lucas chuckled. "So what are you going to do about it?"

Harrison grunted and took a sip of his beer. "I asked her to marry me."

"Whoa," Brayden said. "That's serious."

"When's the wedding?" Dexter asked.

Harrison cursed. "She turned me down."

"Damn," Lucas said.

"Why?" Dexter asked.

"I thought she was crushing on you in high school," Brayden added.

"Mother hasn't made any bones about the way she feels about Honey," Harrison said, his throat rough with emotions. "Honey said she wouldn't come between me and my family."

"Good God, she does love you," Brayden said.

Harrison looked at them in confusion. "Did you hear me? I said she turned me down."

"She wouldn't care so much about your family if she didn't love you," Dexter said.

Harrison rubbed his hand over his eyes. Were his brothers right? Did Honey love him?

If so, how could he convince her to marry him?

He shoved his beer away. "I have to talk to Mother." Then he hurried from the bar. He just hoped he could persuade his mother that she was wrong about Honey.

He didn't want to have to choose between them…

HONEY HAD CRIED herself sick all the way back to Austin. She slipped into her house, the empty walls echoing with loneliness, a reminder of what she'd left behind.

All her life she'd wanted Harrison. Had fantasized about having him touch her, hold her, make love to her.

Had dreamed about being his wife.

Although she thought she'd cried all her tears out, another sob escaped her and the flood began again.

She showered, purging her emotions and praying one day she'd get past the pain of losing Harrison.

But he was the only man she'd ever loved.

And she would never get over him.

# Chapter Twenty-Six

*Two days later*

Honey hung the last of the sketches for Lower Tumbleweed on the wall of the showroom in her home office. The houses were going to be beautiful.

The developer she was working with, a man named Tanner Baldwin, was almost as excited about the project as she was.

Fatigue pulled at her muscles, and she stood and stretched. Everything was going well in her business.

But at night, the empty rooms of her house haunted her.

She missed Harrison so much that her heart literally throbbed.

A knock sounded on the door, and she rushed to answer it. Surprise tightened her chest. Harrison's mother, Mrs. Hawk, entered, her gaze wary as she glanced around the interior of the showroom.

Uncertain what to expect from the woman, Honey simply folded her arms and greeted her. She'd seen the notice for the memorial service for Chrissy and knew the past week had been difficult for the Hawks.

"Hello, Honey," Mrs. Hawk said.

She offered the woman a tentative smile. "Mrs. Hawk."

Mrs. Hawk feathered her hair behind one ear. "We need to talk."

Honey frowned. Was she going to try to stop her from developing that neighborhood? "If this is about the housing development—"

"It is and it's not," Mrs. Hawk said, cutting her off.

"I don't understand," Honey said.

Mrs. Hawk walked over and studied the sketches on the wall. "I saw your plans."

Honey swallowed hard. "What is it you don't approve of, the plans or the fact that I'm developing the neighborhood?"

Mrs. Hawk winced. "I guess I deserve that, but truthfully I think the plans are phenomenal."

Shock slammed into Honey. "Really?"

"Yes, I'm impressed with what you're doing for our town, especially considering how some of the people treated you."

"Some of the people?" Honey said, hurt lacing her voice.

Mrs. Hawk nodded. "Yes, some of them. And I'm aware that includes me."

An awkward silence stretched between them. Honey wanted to fill it, but her emotions got in the way. Besides, she still didn't know the woman's agenda.

And she was certain Mrs. Hawk had one.

"I came to apologize." Mrs. Hawk's voice cracked. "I… I misjudged you."

Honey arched a brow, speechless.

Mrs. Hawk fiddled with the cuff of her satin blouse, obviously nervous. Tense seconds passed.

Honey remained silent, waiting on the other shoe to drop. "What is it you want?"

The woman winced again. "Like I said, I came to apologize. I was harsh toward you when you lived in Lower Tumbleweed." She paused and fidgeted. "But I had my reasons."

She'd driven all the way to Austin to justify her behavior. "I know, I wasn't good enough for your family." Honey sighed. "You didn't need to come here to tell me that again."

"That's not exactly it." Mrs. Hawk dropped her purse onto the conference table where Honey usually met with clients.

"Then what is it?"

Mrs. Hawk inhaled sharply. "When you were a teenager, you reminded me of myself."

Honey stared at her in shock. She certainly hadn't expected the woman to say that.

"I had a wild streak in me before I met Steven, the boys' father. In fact, I didn't exactly come from a very nice family myself."

"You didn't?"

Mrs. Hawk shook her head. "No, my mother was the alcoholic, though. She also slept around. And then when Steven and I had trouble, and I had that affair, I was terrified I was going to be like her. So I broke it off with the other man, and Steven and I made amends, and I swore I would make it up to him the rest of our lives."

Honey had never imagined Harrison's mother as anything but the imposing, judgmental woman who'd hated her.

"Anyway, it doesn't make my behavior right, but I wanted my kids to grow up and have everything. Then Chrissy became infatuated with you and I was terrified she'd end up like me or my mother, and I… took it out on you."

"I would never have hurt her," Honey said. "I think she just wanted a big sister."

"I know." Mrs. Hawk's voice cracked. "I've blamed myself for years for her disappearance. I thought that perhaps she'd run off because I was too harsh on her and that's why she was taken from me."

Sympathy for the woman filled Honey. "Chrissy loved you," she said simply. "She wasn't running away from you."

Tears trickled down her cheeks. She wiped them away with trembling hands. "I was wrong and cruel to you. You deserved kindness and understanding, not my judgmental attitude."

Honey bit her bottom lip. She didn't know how to respond.

"Anyway, I don't know if you can ever forgive me, but I realize now that I lost a daughter and have a void in my heart from missing her, and you lost a mother and you might have a void, too."

Honey swallowed hard.

Mrs. Hawk continued, "I admire what you've done here in Austin and what you're doing in Tumbleweed, and I wanted you to know that if you and Harrison want to be together, that you have my approval."

Honey's heart squeezed. "Mrs. Hawk, I care about your son, but—"

"No buts," Mrs. Hawk said. "My son has been miserable the past few days. He loves you, and he's blamed himself long enough for what happened to Chrissy. He deserves to be happy, and if that means marrying you, then that's what I want for him." She gestured toward herself then to Honey. "I just hope that you can find some way to forgive me and we could perhaps even be friends."

The woman held out her hands in an offering, and Honey read the sincerity in her eyes and voice. How could she say no?

"You do love him, don't you?" Mrs. Hawk asked.

Tears blurred Honey's eyes. "Yes."

A smile broadened the woman's face. "Then let's go tell him."

HARRISON DREADED ANOTHER family dinner. Dammit, he was tired of trying to put on a happy face. He missed Honey like crazy.

His brothers had guessed the reason for his sour

mood and his mother had interrogated him, but he'd refused to talk about it.

How could he tell her that she'd run off the love of his life? Although part of him wondered if Honey just didn't love him.

If she did, why hadn't she fought to be with him?

*You know why. She hates Tumbleweed and the people in it.*

Although if she truly hated the town, why was she spending money and time developing that neighborhood for other families to move into? If she hated it, why wouldn't she have simply sold off her father's land and be done with the community?

Did she think she had something to prove to everyone?

He wiped his feet on the mat and went inside the house, surprised that his mother didn't greet him at the door. The funeral had been heart wrenching, but afterward, it almost seemed as if a weight had been lifted from her shoulders.

The burden of not knowing had taken its toll on all of the Hawks.

Brayden, Dexter and Lucas met him in the dining room, and greeted him with a drink. The scent of something cooking—maybe her Crock-Pot chicken stew—wafted to him.

"Where's Mom?"

His brothers shrugged and looked around with vague expressions. Before they could discuss it further, the door opened and his mother's heels clicked on the foyer floor. When she rounded the corner into the dining room, he was surprised to see Honey with her.

He froze, drink midair, mouth agape.

Honey's gaze met his, uncertainty glinting in her eyes.

"We have company tonight," his mother said.

He and his brothers traded confused looks, then his mother waved her hand toward the bar. "Well, where are your manners, boys? Someone get Honey a drink."

A tiny smile tugged at the corner of Honey's mouth. Lucas rushed to the bar. "Wine? Scotch?"

"White wine would be nice," Honey said softly.

Lucas poured her a glass while Harrison stood gaping at her like a lovesick fool. He wanted to swing her up in his arms and carry her upstairs, but she had turned down his proposal, and his pride and heart still ached.

"It will take me a few minutes to get dinner on the table," his mother said. "Harrison, why don't you take Honey outside for some fresh air? I think she has something to say to you."

Honey shrugged. "Maybe this is a bad time."

"This is a fine time," his mother said firmly.

Lucas nudged him. Dexter chuckled and Brayden raised a brow in challenge. He felt like an idiot.

Honey dampened her lips with her tongue, drawing his hungry gaze to her mouth. "Harrison?"

He gathered his wits and gestured toward the front door. "Yes, let's step onto the porch."

Her sweet scent teased at his senses as he followed her to the front porch like a dog in heat.

"If you want me to leave, just say so," she said as she faced him on the porch.

"I don't want you to leave," he said gruffly. "I just wasn't expecting you. Is something wrong?"

She bit down on her lower lip then shook her head slightly. "Your mother came to see me."

Shock slithered through him. "God, Honey, I'm sorry. I had no idea she was going to do that. What in the world did she say to you now?"

A slow smile spread on her beautiful face. "Actually we had a nice talk. She apologized for the way she treated me."

"My mother apologized?"

Honey nodded. "We came to an understanding."

He rubbed his forehead, confused. "What kind of understanding?"

Honey sipped her wine, her gaze hooded as she stepped closer to him. Then she lifted her chin with that stubborn glint that he recognized from childhood. And from their discussions about her father and the investigation.

"An understanding that we both care about you," she said.

His heart picked up a beat.

"In spite of everything, I know my mother loves me," he said, uncertain of her meaning.

She raised one hand and pressed it against his cheek. "So do I, Harrison."

His breath stalled in his chest. Did she mean that?

"Am I too late?" Honey asked. "Have you changed your mind about wanting me?"

A deep laugh rumbled from him, pure surprise, joy and hope, and he swung her up into his arms. "Not a chance."

She fused her mouth with his, and he kissed her so deeply that every cell his body screamed with hunger. "I have to know this is forever, though," he murmured against her ear as they broke the kiss. "I know you hate this town and I don't want you to be unhappy." He pulled away and gazed into her eyes, pouring his love and heart into the words. "I want us to be a family, to get married and have a home and babies. And if that means leaving Tumbleweed, we will."

Honey looped her arms around his neck. "Home is wherever you are, Harrison."

"God, I love you," he growled.

"I love you, too."

He wrapped his arms around her and kissed her again.

"And you'll marry me?" he murmured.

Moonlight played off her eyes, which sparkled with affection. "Yes, Harrison, I'll marry you."

He reached inside his pocket and retrieved the ring that he'd bought her. He'd considered returning it, but had held on to it just as he'd held on to hope that one day she'd change her mind and have him.

He knelt on one knee, took her hand in his and slid the diamond onto her finger.

Tears slipped down her cheeks, but her radiant smile told him they were tears of happiness.

The front door swung open then, and his brothers appeared. "What's going on?" Brayden asked.

Harrison scooped Honey into his arms, swung her around, joy overflowing from both of them.

"I'm marrying Honey Granger," he shouted.

His mother appeared then, a smile on her face. "It's about time we had a wedding at Hawk's Landing."

He looked at Honey for confirmation, and she kissed him and murmured, "Yes." His brothers cheered and congratulated them, and Harrison hugged his mother.

Finally the dark days were over for the Hawks. A new chapter was starting, and he and Honey would make their own family and create new, happy memories together.

Memories that would bring Hawk's Landing back to life again just the way Honey had brought new life back to him.

Memories that would last forever.

\* \* \* \* \*